TWO WORLDS OF RAYMOND F. JONES

TWO WORLDS OF RAYMOND F. JONES

RAYMOND F. JONES

The Memory of Mars

and

Cubs of the Wolf

WILDSIDE PRESS

TWO WORLDS OF RAYMOND F. JONES

"The Memory of Mars" originally appeared in the
December, 1961 issue of *Amazing Stories*. "Cubs of the
Wolf" originally appeared in the November 1955 issue
of *Astounding Science Fiction*.

CONTENTS

THE MEMORY OF MARS

A reporter should be objective even about a hospital. It's his business to stir others' emotions and not let his own be stirred. But that was no good, Mel Hastings told himself. No good at all when it was Alice who was here somewhere, balanced uncertainly between life and death.

Alice had been in Surgery far too long. Something had gone wrong. He was sure of it. He glanced at his watch. It would soon be dawn outside. To Mel Hastings this marked a significant and irrevocable passage of time. If Alice were to emerge safe and whole from the white cavern of Surgery she would have done so now.

Mel sank deeper in the heavy chair, feeling a quietness within himself as if the slow creep of death were touching him also. There was a sudden far distant roar and through the window he saw a streak of brightness in the sky. That would be the tourist ship, the Martian Princess, he remembered.

That was the last thing Alice had said before they took her away from him. "As soon as I'm well again we'll go to Mars for a vacation again, and then you'll remember. It's so beautiful there. We had so much fun—"

Funny, wonderful little Alice—and her strange delusion that she still clung to, that they had taken a

Martian vacation in the first year of their marriage. It had started about a year ago, and nothing he could say would shake it. Neither of them had ever been to space.

He wished now he had taken her. It would have been worth it, no matter what its personal cost. He had never told her about the phobia that had plagued him all his life, the fear of outer space that made him break out in a cold sweat just to think of it—nor of the nightmare that came again and again, ever since he was a little boy.

There must have been some way to lick this thing—to give her that vacation on Mars that she had wanted so much.

Now it was too late. He knew it was too late.

The white doors opened, and Dr. Winters emerged slowly. He looked at Mel Hastings a long time as if trying to remember who the reporter was. "I must see you—in my office," he said finally.

Mel stared back in numb recognition. "She's dead," he said.

Dr. Winters nodded slowly as if in surprise and wonder that Mel had divined this fact. "I must see you in my office," he repeated.

Mel watched his retreating figure. There seemed no point in following. Dr. Winters had said all that need be said. Far down the corridor the Doctor turned and stood patiently as if understanding why Mel had not followed, but determined to wait until he did. The reporter stirred and rose from the chair, his legs withering beneath him. The figure of Dr. Winters grew larger as he approached. The morning clatter of the hospital seemed an ear-torturing shrillness. The door of the office closed and shut it out.

"She is dead." Dr. Winters sat behind the desk and folded and unfolded his hands. He did not look at Mel. "We did everything we could, Mr. Hastings. Her injuries from the accident were comparatively minor—" He hesitated, then went on. "In normal circumstances there would have been no question—her injuries could have been repaired."

"What do you mean, 'In normal circumstances—'?"

Dr. Winters turned his face away from Mel for a moment as if to avoid some pain beyond endurance. He passed a weary hand across his forehead and eyes and held it there a moment before speaking. Then he faced Mel again. "The woman you brought in here last night—your wife—is completely un-normal in her internal structure. Her internal organs cannot even be identified. She is like a being of some other species. She is not—she is simply not human, Mr. Hastings."

Mel stared at him, trying to grasp the meaning of the words. Meaning would not come. He uttered a short, hysterical laugh that was like a bark. "You're crazy, Doc. You've completely flipped your lid!"

Dr. Winters nodded. "For hours during the night I was in agreement with that opinion. When I first observed your wife's condition I was convinced I was utterly insane. I called in six other men to verify my observation. All of them were as stupefied as I by what we saw. Organs that had no place in a human structure. Evidence of a chemistry that existed in no living being we had ever seen before—"

The Doctor's words rolled over him like a roaring surf, burying, smothering, destroying—

"I want to see." Mel's voice was like a hollow

cough from far away. "I think you're crazy. I think you're hiding some mistake you made yourself. You killed Alice in a simple little operation, and now you're trying to get out of it with some crazy story that nobody on earth would ever believe!"

"I want you to see," said Dr. Winters, rising slowly. "That's why I called you in here, Mr. Hastings."

Mel trailed him down the long corridor again. No words were spoken between them. Mel felt as if nothing were real anymore.

They went through the white doors of Surgery and through the inner doors. Then they entered a white, silent—cold—room beyond.

In the glare of icy white lights a single sheeted figure rested on a table. Mel suddenly didn't want to see. But Dr. Winters was drawing back the cover. He exposed the face, the beloved features of Alice Hastings. Mel cried out her name and moved toward the table. There was nothing in her face to suggest she was not simply sleeping, her hair disarrayed, her face composed and relaxed as he had seen her hundreds of times.

"Can you stand to witness this?" asked Dr. Winters anxiously. "Shall I get you a sedative?"

Mel shook his head numbly. "No—show me ..."

The great, fresh wound extended diagonally across the abdomen and branched up beneath the heart. The Doctor grasped a pair of small scissors and swiftly clipped the temporary sutures. With forceps and retractors he spread open the massive incision.

Mel closed his eyes against the sickness that seized

him.

"Gangrene!" he said. "She's full of gangrene!"

Below the skin, the surface layers of fatty tissue, the substance of the tissue changed from the dark red of the wounded tissue to a dark and greenish hue that spoke of deadly decay.

But Dr. Winters was shaking his head. "No. It's not gangrene. That's the way we found the tissue. That appears to be its—normal condition, if you will."

Mel stared without believing, without comprehending.

Dr. Winters probed the wound open further. "We should see the stomach here," he said. "What is here where the stomach should be I cannot tell you. There is no name for this organ. The intestinal tract should lie here. Instead, there is only this homogeneous mass of greenish, gelatinous material. Other organs, hardly differentiated from this mass, appear where the liver, the pancreas, the spleen should be."

Mel was hearing his voice as if from some far distance or in a dream.

"There are lungs—of a sort," the Doctor went on. "She was certainly capable of breathing. And there's a greatly modified circulatory system, two of them, it appears. One circulates a blood substance in the outer layers of tissue that is almost normal. The other circulates a liquid that gives the remainder of the organs their greenish hue. But how circulation takes place we do not know. She has no heart."

Mel Hastings burst out in hysterical laughter. "Now I know you're crazy Doc! My tender, loving Alice with no heart! She used to tell me, 'I haven't got any brains. I wouldn't have married a dumb reporter if I did. But so I've got a heart and that's what fell in love with you—my heart, not my brains.' She loved me, can't you understand that?"

Dr. Winters was slowly drawing him away. "I understand. Of course I understand. Come with me now, Mr. Hastings, and lie down for a little while. I'll get you something to help take away the shock."

Mel permitted himself to be led away to a small room nearby. He drank the liquid the Doctor brought, but he refused to lie down.

"You've shown me," he said with dull finality. "But I don't care what the explanation is. I knew Alice. She was human all right, more so than either you or I. She was completely normal, I tell you—all except for this idea she had the last year or so that we'd gone together on a vacation to Mars at one time."

"That wasn't true?"

"No. Neither of us had ever been out in space."

"How well did you know your wife before you married her?"

Mel smiled in faint reminiscence. "We grew up together, went to the same grade school and high school. It seems like there was never a time when Alice and I didn't know each other. Our folks lived next door for years."

"Was she a member of a large family?"

"She had an older brother and sister and two younger sisters."

"What were her parents like?"

"They're still living. Her father runs an implement store. It's a farm community where they live. Wonderful people. Alice was just like them."

Dr. Winters was silent before he went on. "I have subjected you to this mental torture for just one reason, Mr. Hastings. If it has been a matter of any less importance I would not have told you the details of your wife's condition, much less asking you to look at her. But this is such an enormous scientific mystery that I must ask your cooperation in helping to solve it. I want your permission to preserve and dissect the body of your wife for the cause of science."

Mel looked at the Doctor in sudden sharp antagonism. "Not even give her a burial? Let her be put away in bottles, like—like a—"

"Please don't upset yourself any more than necessary. But I do beg that you consider what I've just proposed. Surely a moment's reflection will show you that this is no more barbaric than our other customs regarding our dead.

"But even this is beside the point. The girl, Alice, whom you married is like a normal human being in every apparent external respect, yet the organs which gave her life and enabled her to function are like nothing encountered before in human experience. It is imperative that we understand the meaning of this. It is yours to say whether or not we shall have this opportunity."

Mel started to speak again, but the words wouldn't come out.

"Time is critical," said Dr. Winters, "but I don't want to force you to an instantaneous answer. Take thirty minutes to think about it. Within that time, additional means of preservation must be taken. I regret that I must be in such haste, but I urge that your answer be yes."

Dr. Winters moved towards the door, but Mel gestured for him to remain.

"I want to see her again," Mel said.

"There is no need. You have been tortured

enough. Remember your wife as you have known her all her life, not as you saw her a moment ago."

"If you want my answer let me see her again."

Dr. Winters led the way silently back to the cold room. Mel drew down the cover only far enough to expose the face of Alice. There was no mistake. Somehow he had been hoping that all this would turn out to be some monstrous error. But there was no error.

Would she want me to do what the Doctor has asked? he thought. She wouldn't care. She would probably think it a very huge joke that she had been born with innards that made her different from everybody else. She would be amused by the profound probings and mutterings of the learned doctors trying to find an explanation for something that had no explanation.

Mel drew the sheet tenderly over her face.

"You can do as you wish," he said to Dr. Winters. "It makes no difference to us—to either of us."

The sedative Dr. Winters had given him, plus his own exhaustion, drove Mel to sleep for a few hours during the afternoon, but by evening he was awake again and knew that a night of sleeplessness lay ahead of him. He couldn't stand to spend it in the house, with all its fresh reminders of Alice.

He walked out into the street as it began to get dark. Walking was easy; almost no one did it any more. The rush of private and commercial cars swarmed overhead and rumbled in the ground beneath. He was an isolated anachronism walking silently at the edge of the great city.

He was sick of it. He would have liked to have

turned his back on the city and left it forever. Alice had felt the same. But there was nowhere to go. News reporting was the only thing he knew, and news occurred only in the great, ugly cities of the world. The farmlands, such as he and Alice had known when they were young, produced nothing of interest to the satiated denizens of the towns and cities. Nothing except food, and much of this was now being produced by great factories that synthesized protein and carbohydrates. When fats could be synthesized the day of the farmer would be over.

He wondered if there weren't some way out of it now. With Alice gone there was only himself, and his needs were few. He didn't know, but suddenly he wanted very much to see it all again. And, besides, he had to tell her folks.

The ancient surface bus reached Central Valley at noon the next day. It all looked very much as it had the last time Mel had seen it and it looked very good indeed. The vast, open lands; the immense ripe fields.

The bus passed the high school where Mel and Alice had attended classes together. He half expected to see her running across the campus lawn to meet him. In the middle of town he got off the bus and there were Alice's mother and father.

They were dry-eyed now but white and numb with shock. George Dalby took his hand and pumped it heavily. "We can't realize it, Mel. We just can't believe Alice is gone."

His wife put her arms around Mel and struggled

with her tears again. "You didn't say anything about the funeral. When will it be?"

Mel swallowed hard, fighting the one lie he had to tell. He almost wondered now why he had agreed to Dr. Winters' request. "Alice—always wanted to do all the good she could in the world," he said. "She figured that she could be of some use even after she was gone. So she made an agreement with the research hospital that they could have her body after she died."

It took a moment for her mother to grasp the meaning. Then she cried out, "We can't even bury her?"

"We should have a memorial service, right here at home where all her friends are," said Mel.

George Dalby nodded in his grief. "That was just like Alice," he said. "Always wanting to do something for somebody else—"

And it was true, Mel thought. If Alice had supposed she was not going to live any longer she would probably have thought of the idea, herself. Her parents were easily reconciled.

They took him out to the old familiar house and gave him the room where he and Alice had spent the first days of their marriage.

When it was night and the lights were out he felt able to sleep naturally for the first time since Alice's accident. She seemed not far away here in this old familiar house.

In memory, she was not, for Mel was convinced he could remember the details of his every association with her. He first became conscious of her existence one day when they were in the third grade. At the beginning of each school year the younger pupils went through a course of weighing, inspection, knee tapping, and cavity counting. Mel had come in late for his examination that year and barged into the wrong room. A shower of little-girl squeals had greeted him as the teacher told him kindly where the boy's examination room was.

But he remembered most vividly Alice Dalby standing in the middle of the room, her blouse off but held protectingly in front of her as she jumped up and down in rage and pointed a finger at him. "You get out of here, Melvin Hastings! You're not a nice boy at all!"

Face red, he had hastily retreated as the teacher assured Alice and the rest of the girls that he had made a simple mistake. But how angry Alice had been! It was a week before she would speak to him.

He smiled and sank back deeply into the pillow. He remembered how proud he had been when old Doc Collins, who came out to do the honors every Fall, had told him there wasn't a thing wrong with him and that if he continued to drink his milk regularly he'd grow up to be a football player. He could still hear Doc's words whistling through his teeth and feel the coldness of the stethoscope on his chest.

Suddenly, he sat upright in bed in the darkness.

Stethoscope!

They had tapped and inspected and listened to Alice that day, and all the other examination days.

If Doc Collins had been unable to find a heartbeat in her he'd have fainted—and spread the news all over town!

Mel got up and stood at the window, his heart pounding. Old Doc Collins was gone, but the medical records of those school examinations might still be around somewhere. He didn't know what he expected to prove, but surely those records would not tell the same story Dr. Winters had told.

It took him nearly all the next day. The grade school principal agreed to help him check through the dusty attic of the school, where ancient records and papers were tumbled about and burst from their cardboard boxes.

Then Paul Ames, the school board secretary, took Mel down to the District Office and offered to help look for the records. The old building was stifling hot and dusty with summer disuse. But down in the cool, cobwebbed basement they found it.... Alice's records from the third grade on up through the ninth. On every one: heart, o.k.; lungs, normal. Pulse and blood pressure readings were on each chart.

"I'd like to take these," said Mel. "Her doctor in town—he wants to write some kind of paper on her case and would like all the past medical history he can get."

Paul Ames frowned thoughtfully. "I'm not allowed to give District property away. But they should have been thrown out a long time ago—take 'em and don't tell anybody I let you have 'em."

"Thanks. Thanks a lot," Mel said.

And when she was fourteen or fifteen her appendix had been removed. A Dr. Brown had performed the operation, Mel remembered. He had taken over from Collins.

"Sure, he's still here," Paul Ames said. "Same office old Doc Collins used. You'll probably find him there right now."

Dr. Brown remembered. He didn't remember the

details of the appendectomy, but he still had records that showed a completely normal operation.

"I wonder if I could get a copy of that record and have you sign it," Mel said. He explained about the interest of Dr. Winters in her case without revealing the actual circumstances.

"Glad to," said Dr. Brown. "I just wish things hadn't turned out the way they have. One of the loveliest girls that ever grew up here, Alice."

The special memorial service was held in the old community church on Sunday afternoon. It was like the drawing of a curtain across a portion of Mel's life, and he knew that curtain would never open again.

He took a bus leaving town soon after the service.

There was one final bit of evidence, and he wondered all the way back to town why he had not thought of it first. Alice's pregnancy had ended in miscarriage, and there had never been another.

But X-rays had been taken to try to find the cause of Alice's difficulty. If they showed that Alice was normal within the past two years—

Dr. Winters was mildly surprised to see Mel again. He invited the reporter in to his office and offered him a chair. "I suppose you have come to inquire about our findings regarding your wife."

"Yes—if you've found anything," said Mel. "I've got a couple of things to show you."

"We've found little more than we knew the night of her death. We have completed the dissection of the body. A minute analysis of each organ is now under way, and chemical tests of the body's substances are being made. We found that differences in the skeletal structure were almost as great as those in the fleshy tissues. We find no relationship between these structures and those of any other species—human or animal—that we have ever found."

"And yet Alice was not always like that," said Mel.

Dr. Winters looked at him sharply. "How do you know that?"

Mel extended the medical records he had obtained in Central Valley. Dr. Winters picked them up and examined them for a long time while Mel watched silently.

Finally, Dr. Winters put the records down with a sigh. "This seems to make the problem even more complex than it was."

"There are X-rays, too," said Mel. "Alice had pelvic X-rays only a little over two years ago. I tried to get them, but the doctor said you'd have to request them. They should be absolute proof that Alice was different then."

"Tell me who has them and I'll send for them at once."

An hour later Dr. Winters shook his head in disbelief as he turned off the light box and removed the X-ray photograph. "It's impossible to believe that these were taken of your wife, but they corroborate the evidence of the other medical records. They show a perfectly normal structure."

The two men remained silent across the desk, each reluctant to express his confused thoughts. Dr.

Winters finally broke the silence. "It must be, Mr. Hastings," he said, "—it must be that this woman—this utterly alien person—is simply not your wife, Alice. Somehow, somewhere, there must be a mistake in identity, a substitution of similar individuals."

"She was not out of my sight," said Mel. "Everything was completely normal when I came home that night. Nothing was out of place. We went out to a show. Then, on the way home, the accident occurred. There could have been no substitution—except right here in the hospital. But I know it was Alice I saw. That's why I made you let me see her again—to make sure."

"But the evidence you have brought me proves otherwise. These medical records, these X-rays prove that the girl, Alice, whom you married, was quite normal. It is utterly impossible that she could have metamorphosed into the person on whom we operated."

Mel stared at the reflection of the sky in the polished desk top. "I don't know the answer," he said. "It must not be Alice. But if that's the case, where is Alice?"

"That might even be a matter for the police," said Dr. Winters. "There are many things yet to be learned about this mystery."

"There's one thing more," said Mel. "Fingerprints. When we first came here Alice got a job where she had to have her fingerprints taken."

"Excellent!" Dr. Winters exclaimed. "That should give us our final proof!"

It took the rest of the afternoon to get the fingerprint record and make a comparison. Dr. Winters called Mel at home to give him the report. There was no question. The fingerprints were identical. The corpse was that of Alice Hastings.

The nightmare came again that night. Worse than Mel could ever remember it. As always, it was a dream of space, black empty space, and he was floating alone in the immense depths of it. There was no direction. He was caught in a whirlpool of vertigo from which he reached out with agonized yearning for some solidarity to cling to.

There was only space.

After a time he was no longer alone. He could not see them, but he knew they were out there. The searchers. He did not know why he had to flee or why they sought him, but he knew they must never overtake him, or all would be lost.

Somehow he found a way to propel himself through empty space. The searchers were growing points of light in the far distance. They gave him a sense of direction. His being, his existence, his universe of meaning and understanding depended on the success of his flight from the searchers. Faster, through the wild black depths of space—

He never knew whether he escaped or not. Always he awoke in a tangle of bedclothes, bathed in sweat, whimpering in fear. For a long time Alice had been there to touch his hand when he awoke. But Alice was gone now and he was so weary of the night pursuit. Sometimes he wished it would end with the searchers—whoever they were—catching up with him and doing what they intended to do. Then maybe there would be no more nightmare. Maybe there would be no more Mel Hastings, he thought. And that wouldn't be so bad, either.

He tossed sleeplessly the rest of the night and got up at dawn feeling as if he had not been to bed at all. He would take one day more, and then get back to the News Bureau. He'd take this day to do what couldn't be put off any longer—the collecting and disposition of Alice's personal belongings.

He shaved, bathed and dressed, then began emptying the drawers, one by one. There were many souvenirs, mementos. She was always collecting these. Her bottom drawer was full of stuff that he'd glimpsed only occasionally.

In the second layer of junk in the drawer he came across the brochure on Martian vacations. It must have been one of the dreams of her life, he thought. She'd wanted it so much that she'd almost come to believe that it was real. He turned the pages of the smooth, glossy brochure. Its cover bore the picture of the great Martian Princess and the blazoned emblem of Connemorra Space Lines. Inside were glistening photos of the plush interior of the great vacation liner, and pictures of the domed cities of Mars where Earthmen played more than they worked. Mars had become the great resort center of Earth.

Mel closed the book and glanced again at the Connemorra name. Only one man had ever amassed the resources necessary to operate a private space line. Jim Connemorra had done it; no one knew quite how. But he operated now out of both hemispheres with a space line that ignored freight and dealt only in passenger business. He made money, on a scale that no government-operated line had yet been able to approach.

Mel sank down to the floor, continuing to shift through the other things in the drawer.

His hand stopped. He remained motionless as recognition showered sudden frantic questions in his mind. There lay a ticket envelope marked *Connemorra Lines*.

The envelope was empty when he looked inside, and there was no name on it. But it was worn. As if it might have been carried to Mars and back.

In sudden frenzy he began examining each article and laying it in a careless pile on the floor. He recognized a pair of idiotic Martian dolls. He found a tourist map of the ruined cities of Mars. He found a menu from the Red Sands Hotel.

And below all these there was a picture album. Alice at the Red Sands. Alice at the Phobos Oasis. Alice at the Darnella Ruins. He turned the pages of the album with numb fingers. Alice in a dozen Martian settings. Some of them were dated. About two years ago. They had gone together, Alice had said, but there was no evidence of Mel's presence on any such trip.

But it was equally impossible that Alice had made the trip, yet here was proof. Proof that swept him up in a doubting of his own senses. How could such a thing have taken place? Had he actually made such a trip and been stripped of the memory by some amnesia? Maybe he had forced himself to go with her and the power of his lifelong phobia had wiped it from his memory.

And what did it all have to do—if anything—with

the unbelievable thing Dr. Winters had found about Alice?

Overcome with grief and exhaustion he sat fingering the mementos aimlessly while he stared at the pictures and the ticket envelope and the souvenirs.

D r. Winters spoke a little more sharply than he intended. "I don't think anything is going to be solved by a wild-goose chase to Mars. It's going to cost you a great deal of money, and there isn't a single positive lead to any solution."

"It's the only possible explanation." Mel persisted. "Something happened on Mars to change her from what she once was to—what you saw on your operating table."

"And you are hoping that in some desperate way you will find there was a switch of personalities—that there may be a ghost of a chance of finding Alice still alive."

Mel bit his lip. He was scarcely willing to admit such a hope but it was the foundation of his decision. "I've got to do what I can," he said. "I must take the chance. The uncertainty will torment me all my life if I don't."

Dr. Winters shook his head. "I still wish I could persuade you against it. You will find only disappointment."

"My mind is made up. Will you help me or not?"

"What can I do?"

"I can't go into space unless I can find some way of lifting, even temporarily, this phobia that nearly drives me crazy at the thought of going out there. Isn't there a drug, a hypnotic method, or something to help a thing like this?"

"This isn't my field," said Dr. Winters. "But I suspect that the cause of your trouble cannot be suppressed. It will have to be lifted. Psycho-recovery is the only way to accomplish that. I can recommend a number of good men. This, too, is very expensive."

"I should have done it for Alice—long ago," said Mel.

D r. Martin, the psychiatrist, was deeply interested in Mel's problem. "It sounds as if it is based on some early trauma, which has long since been wiped from your conscious memory. Recovery may be easy or difficult, depending on how much suppression of the original event has taken place."

"I don't even care what the original event was," said Mel, "if you rid me of this overwhelming fear of space. Dr. Winters said he thought recovery would be required."

"He is right. No matter how much overlay you pile on top of such a phobia to suppress it, it will continue to haunt you. We can make a trial run to analyze the situation, and then we can better predict the chance of ultimate success."

As a reporter, Mel Hastings had had vague encounters with the subject of psycho-recovery, but he knew little of the details about it. He knew it involved some kind of a machine that could tap the very depths of the human mind and drag out the hidden debris accumulated in mental basements and attics. But such things had always given him the willies. He steered clear of them.

When Dr. Martin first introduced him into the psycho-recovery room his resolution almost vanished. It looked more like a complex electronic laboratory than anything else. A half dozen operators and assistants in nurses' uniforms stood by.

"If you will recline here—," Dr. Martin was saying.

Mel felt as if he were being prepared for some inhuman biological experiment. A cage of terminals was fitted to his head and a thousand small electrodes adjusted to contact with his skull. The faint hum of equipment supported the small surge of apprehension within him.

After half an hour the preparations were complete. The level of lights in the room was lowered. He could sense the operators at their panels and see dimly the figure of Dr. Martin seated near him.

"Try to recall as vividly as possible your last experience with this nightmare you have described. We will try to lock on to that and follow it on down."

This was the last thing in the world Mel wanted to do. He lay in agonized indecision, remembering that he had dreamed only a short time ago, but fighting off the actual recollection of the dream.

"Let yourself go," Dr. Martin said kindly. "Don't fight it—"

A fragment of his mind let down its guard for a brief instant. It was like touching the surface of a whirlpool. He was sucked into the sweeping depths of the dream. He sensed that he cried out in terror as he plunged. But there was no one to hear. He was alone in space.

Fear wrapped him like black, clammy fur. He felt

the utter futility of even being afraid. He would simply remain as he was, and soon he would cease to be.

But they were coming again. He sensed, rather than saw them. The searchers. And his fear of them was greater than his fear of space alone. He moved. Somehow he moved, driving headlong through great vastness while the pinpoints of light grew behind him.

"Very satisfactory," Dr. Martin was saying. "An extremely satisfactory probe."

His voice came through to Mel as from beyond vast barriers of time and space. Mel felt the thick sweat that covered his body. Weakness throbbed in his muscles.

"It gives us a very solid anchor point," Dr. Martin said. "From here I think we run back to the beginning of the experience and unearth the whole thing. Are you ready, Mr. Hastings?"

Mel felt too weak to nod. "Let 'er rip!" he muttered weakly.

The day was warm and sunny. He and Alice had arrived early at the spaceport to enjoy the holiday excitement preceding the takeoff. It was something they had both dreamed of since they were kids—a vacation in the fabulous domed cities and ruins of Mars.

Alice was awed by her first close view of the magnificent ship lying in its water berth that opened to Lake Michigan. "It's *huge*—how can such an enormous ship ever get off the Earth?"

Mel laughed. "Let's not worry about that. We

know it does. That's all that matters." But he could not help being impressed, too, by the enormous size and the graceful lines of the luxury ship. Unlike Alice, he was not seeing it at close range for the first time. He had met the ship scores of times in his reporting job, interviewing famous and well-known personages as they departed or arrived from the fabulous playgrounds of Mars.

"If you look carefully," Mel pointed out, "you'll see a lot of faces that make news when they come and go."

Alice's face glowed as she clung to Mel's arm and recognized some of the famous citizens who would be their fellow passengers. "This is going to be the most fun we've ever had in our lives, darling."

"Like a barrel of monkeys," Mel said casually, enjoying the bubbling excitement that was in Alice.

The ship was so completely stabilized that the passengers did not even have to sit down during takeoff. They crowded the ports to watch the land and the water shoot past as the ship skimmed half the length of Lake Michigan in its takeoff run. As it bore into the upper atmosphere on an ever-increasing angle of climb, its own artificial gravity system took over and gave the illusion of horizontal flight with the Earth receding slowly behind.

Mel and Alice wandered through the salons and along the spacious decks as if in some fairyland-come-true. All sense of time seemed to vanish and they floated with the great ship in timeless, endless space.

He wasn't quite certain when he first became aware of his own sense of disquietude. It seemed to result from a change in the members of the crew. On the morning of the third day they ceased their universal and uninterrupted concern for their passengers' entertainment and enjoyment.

Most of the passengers seemed to have taken no note of it. Mel commented to Alice. She laughed at him. "What do you expect? They've spent two full days showing us the ship and teaching us to play all the games aboard. You don't expect them to play nurse to us during the whole trip, do you?"

It sounded reasonable. "I suppose so," said Mel dubiously. "But just what *are* they doing? They all seem to be in such a hurry to get somewhere this morning."

"Well, they must have some duties to perform in connection with running the ship."

Mel shook his head in doubt.

A lice joined him in wandering about the decks, kibitzing on the games of the other passengers, and watching the stars and galaxies on the telescopic screens. It was on one of these that they first saw the shadow out in space. Small at first, the black shadow crossed a single star and made it wink. That was what caught Mel's attention, a winking star in the dead night of space.

When he was sure, he called Alice's attention to it. "There's something moving out there." By now it had shape, like a tiny black bullet.

"Where? I don't see anything."

"It's crossing that patch of stars. Watch, and you can see it blot them out as it moves."

"It's another ship!" Alice exclaimed. "That's exciting! To think we're passing another ship in all this great emptiness of space! I wonder where it's coming from?"

"And where it's going to."

They watched its slow, precise movement across the stars. After several minutes a steward passed by. Mel hailed him and pointed to the screen. "Can you tell us what that other ship is?"

The steward glanced and seemed to recognize it instantly. But he paused in replying. "That's the Mars liner," he said finally. "In just a few minutes the public address system will announce contact and change of ship."

"Change of ship?" Mel asked, puzzled. "I never heard anything about a change of ship."

"Oh, yes," the steward said. "This is only the shuttle that we're on now. We transfer to the liner for the remainder of the trip. I'm sure that was explained to you at the time you purchased your tickets." He hurried away.

Mel was quite sure no such thing had been explained to him when he purchased tickets. He turned back to the screen and watched the black ship growing swiftly larger now as it and the Martian Princess approached on contact courses.

The public address system came alive suddenly. "This is your Captain. All passengers will now prepare to leave the shuttle and board the Mars liner. Hand luggage should be made ready. All luggage stowed in the hold will be transferred without your attention. It has been a pleasure to have you aboard. Contact with the liner will be made in fifteen minutes."

From the buzz around him Mel knew that this was

as much a surprise to everyone else as it was to him, but it was greeted with excitement and without question.

Even Alice was growing excited now and others crowded around them when it was discovered what they were viewing. "It looks *big*," said Alice in subdued voice. "Bigger than this ship by far."

Mel moved away and let the others have his place before the screen. His sense of uneasiness increased as he contemplated the approach of that huge black ship. And he was convinced its color *was* black, that it was not just the monotone of the view screen that made it so.

Why should there be such a transfer of passengers in mid-space? The Martian Princess was certainly adequate to make the journey to Mars. Actually they were more than a third of the way there, already. He wasn't sure why he felt so certain something was amiss. Surely there was no possibility that the great Connemorra Lines would plan any procedure to the detriment of the more than five thousand passengers aboard the ship. His uneasiness was pretty stupid, he thought.

But it wouldn't go away.

He returned to the crowd clustered at the viewing screen and took Alice by the arm to draw her away.

She looked quizzically at him. "This is the most exciting thing yet. I want to watch it."

"We haven't got much time," Mel said. "We've got a lot of things to get in our suitcases. Let's go down to our stateroom."

"Everyone else has to pack, too. There's no hurry."

"Fifteen minutes, the Captain said. We don't want to be the last ones."

Unwillingly, Alice followed. Their stateroom was a long way from the salon. The fifteen minutes were almost up by the time they reached it.

Mel closed the door to their room and put his hands on Alice's shoulders. He glanced about warily. "Alice—I don't want to go aboard that ship. There's something wrong about this whole thing. I don't know what it is, but we're not going aboard."

Alice stared at him. "Have you lost your mind? After all our hopes and all our planning you don't want to go on to Mars?"

Mel felt as if a wall had suddenly sprung up between them. He clutched Alice's shoulders desperately in his hands. "Alice—I don't think that ship out there is going to Mars. I know it sounds crazy, but please listen to me—we weren't told anything about the Martian Princess being merely a shuttle and that we'd transfer to another ship out here. No one was told. The Martian Princess is a space liner perfectly capable of going to Mars. There's no reason why such a huge ship should be used merely as a shuttle."

"That ship out there is bigger."

"Why? Do we need any more room to finish the journey?"

Alice shook herself out of his grasp. "I don't know the answers to those questions and I don't care to know them!" she said angrily.

"If you think I'm going to give up this vacation and turn right around here in space and go back home you're crazy. If you go back you'll go back alone!"

Alice whirled and ran to the door. Mel ran after her, but she was through the door and was melting into the moving throng by the time he reached the door. He took a step to follow, then halted. He couldn't drag her forcibly back into the stateroom. Maybe she'd return in a few minutes to pack her bags. He went back in the room and closed the door.

Even as he did so he knew that he was guessing wrong. Alice would be matching him in a game of nerves. She'd go on to the other ship, expecting him to pack the bags and follow. He sat down on the bed and put his head in his hands for a moment. A faint shudder passed through the ship and he heard the hollow ring of clashing metal. The unknown ship had made contact with the Martian Princess. Their airlocks were being mated now.

From the porthole he could see the incredible mass of the ship. He crossed the room and pressed the curtains aside. His impression had been right. The ship *was* black. Black, nameless, and blind. No insignia or portholes were visible anywhere on the hull within his range of vision.

He didn't know what he was going to do, but he knew above all else that he wasn't going to board that ship. He paced the floor telling himself it was a stupid, neurotic apprehension that filled his mind, that the great Connemorra Lines could not be involved in any nefarious acts involving five thousand people—or even one person. They couldn't afford such risk.

He couldn't shake it. He was certain that, no matter what the cost, he was not going to board that black ship.

He looked about the stateroom. He couldn't remain here. They'd certainly find him. He had to hide somewhere. He stood motionless, staring out the porthole. There was no place he could hide with assurance inside the ship.

But what about outside?

His thoughts crumpled in indecision as he thought of Alice. Yet whatever the black ship meant, he could help no one if he went aboard. He had to get back to Earth and try to find out what it was all about and alert the authorities. Only in that way could he hope to help Alice.

He opened the stateroom door cautiously and stepped out. The corridor was filled with hurrying passengers, carrying hand luggage, laughing with each other in excitement. He joined them, moving slowly, alert for crew members. There seemed to be none of the latter in the corridors.

Keeping close to the wall, he moved with the crowd until he reached the rounded niche that marked an escape chamber. As if pushed by the hurrying throng, he backed into it, the automatic doors opening and closing to receive him.

The chamber was one of scores stationed throughout the ship as required by law. The escape chambers contained space suits for personal exit from the ship in case of emergency. They were never expected to be used. In any emergency requiring abandonment of the vessel it would be as suicidal to go into space in a suit as to remain with the ship. But fusty lawmakers had decreed their necessity, and passengers received a perfunctory briefing in the use of the chambers and the suits—which they promptly forgot.

Mel wrestled now with what he remembered of the instructions. He inspected a suit hanging in its cabinet and then was relieved to find that the instructions were repeated on a panel of the cabinet. Slowly, he donned the suit, following the step by step instructions as he went. He began to sweat profusely from his exertions and from his fear of discovery.

He finally succeeded in getting the cumbersome gear adjusted and fastened without being detected. He did not know if the airlock of the chamber had some kind of alarm that would alert the crew when it was opened. That was a chance he had to take. He discovered that it was arranged so that it could be opened only by a key operated from within the suit. This was obviously to prevent anyone leaving the ship unprotected. Perhaps with this safeguard there was no alarm.

He twisted the lock and entered the chamber. He opened the outer door and faced the night of space.

He would not have believed that anything could be so utterly terrifying. His knees buckled momentarily and left him clinging to the side of the port. Sweat burst anew from every pore. Blindly, he pressed the jet control and forced himself into space.

He arced a short distance along the curve of the ship and then forced himself down into contact with the hull. He clung by foot and hand magnetic pads, sick with nausea and vertigo.

He had believed that by clinging to the outside of the hull he could escape detection and endure the flight back to Earth. In his sickness of body and mind the whole plan now looked like utter folly. He retched and closed his eyes and lay on the hull through the beginning of an eternity.

He had no concept of time. The chronometer in the suit was not working. But it seemed as if many hours had passed when he felt a faint shock pass through the hull beneath him. He felt a momentary elation. The ships had separated. The search for him—if any—had been abandoned.

Slowly he inched his way around the hull to get a glimpse of the black ship. It was still there, standing off a few hundred yards but not moving. Its presence dismayed him. There could be no reason now for the two ships to remain together. The Martian Princess should be turning around for the return to Earth.

Then out of the corner of his eye he saw it. A trace of movement. A gleam of light. Like a small moon it edged up the distant curvature of the hull. Then there were more—a nest of quivering satellites.

Without thought, Mel pressed the jet control and hurled himself into space.

The terror of his first plunge was multiplied by the presence of the searchers. Crewmen of the Martian Princess, he supposed. The absence of the space suit had probably been discovered.

In headlong flight, he became aware of eternity and darkness and loneliness. The sun was a hot, bright disc, but it illuminated nothing. All that his mind clung to for identification of itself and the universe around it was gone. He was like a primeval cell, floating without origin, without purpose, without destination.

Only a glimmer of memory pierced the thick terror with a shaft of rationality. Alice. He must survive for Alice's sake. He must find the way back to Alice—back to Earth.

He looked toward the Martian Princess and the searchers on the hull. He cried out in the soundless dark. The searchers had left the hull and were pursuing him through open space. Their speed far exceeded his. It was futile to run before them—and futile to leave the haven of the Martian Princess. His only chance of survival or success lay in getting to Earth aboard the ship. In a long curve he arced back toward the ship. Instantly, the searchers moved to close in the arc and meet him on a collision course.

He could see them now. They were not crewmen in spacesuits as he had supposed. Rather, the objects—two of them—looked like miniature spaceships. Beams of light bore through space ahead of them, and he suspected they carried other radiations also to detect by radar and infra red.

In the depths of his mind he knew they were not of the Martian Princess. Nor were there any crewmen within them. They were robot craft of some kind, and they had come from the great black ship.

He felt their searching beams upon him and waited for a deadly, blasting burst of heat or killing radiation. He was not prepared for what happened.

They closed swiftly, and the nearest robot came within a dozen feet, matching Mel's own velocity. Suddenly, from a small opening in the machine, a slender metal tentacle whipped out and wrapped about him like the coils of a snake. The second robot approached and added another binding. Mel's arms and legs were pinned. Frantically, he manipulated the jet control in the glove of the suit. This only caused the tentacles to cut deeply and painfully, and threatened to smash the shell of the suit. He cut the jets and admitted the failure of his frantic mission.

In short minutes they were near the ships again. Mel wondered what kind of reprimand the crewmen of the Martian Princess could give him, and what fantastic justification they might offer for their own actions.

But he wasn't being taken toward the Martian Princess. He twisted painfully in the grip of the robot tentacles and confirmed that he was being carried to the black stranger.

Soundlessly, a port slid open and the robots swept him through into the dark interior of the ship. He felt himself dropped on a hard metal floor. The tentacles unwound. Alone, he struggled to his feet and flashed a beam of light from the suit flashlight to the walls about him. Walls, floor and ceiling were an indistinguishable dark gray. He was the only object in the chamber.

While he strained his sight to establish features in the blank metallic surfaces a clipped, foreign voice spoke. "Remove your suit and walk toward the opening in the wall. Do not try to run or attack. You will not be harmed unless you attack."

There was no use refusing. He did as commanded. A bright doorway opened in the wall before him. He walked through.

It reminded him of a medical laboratory. Shelves and cabinets of hand instruments and electronic equipment were about. And in the room three men sat watching the doorway through which he entered. He gazed at the strangers as they at him.

They looked ordinary enough in their white surgeons' smocks. All seemed to be of middle age, with dark hair turning gray at the fringe. One was considerably more muscular than the other two. One leaned to overweight. The third was quite thin. Yet Mel felt himself bristling like a dog in the dark of the moon.

No matter how ordinary they looked, these three

were not men of Earth. The certainty of this settled like a cold, dead weight in the pit of his stomach.

"You—" he stammered. There was nothing to say.

"Please recline on this couch," the nearest, the muscular one said. "We wish you no harm so do not be afraid. We wish only to determine if you have been harmed by your flight into space."

All three of them were tense and Mel was sure they were worried—by his escapade. Had he nearly let some unknown cat out of the bag?

"Please—," the muscular one said.

He had no alternative. He might struggle, and destroy a good deal of apparatus, but he could not hope to overwhelm them. He lay on the couch as directed. Almost instantly the overweight one was behind him, seizing his arm. He felt the sting of a needle. The thin one was at his feet, looking down at him soberly. "He will rest," the thin one said, "and then we shall know what needs to be done."

The sleep had lasted for an eon, he thought. He had a sense of the passage of an enormous span of time when he at last awoke. His vision was fuzzy, but there was no mistaking the image before him.

Alice. His Alice—safe.

She was sitting on the edge of the bed, smiling down at him. He fought his way up to a half-sitting position. "Alice!" He wept.

Afterwards, he said, "Where are we? What happened? I remember so many crazy things—the vacation to Mars."

"Don't try to remember it all, darling," she said.

"You were sick. Some kind of hysteria and amnesia hit you while we were there. We're home now. You'll soon be out of the hospital and everything will be all right."

"I spoiled it," he murmured. "I spoiled it all for you."

"No. I knew you were going to be all right. I even had a lot of fun all by myself. But we're going back. As soon as you are all well again we'll start saving up and go again."

He nodded drowsily. "Sure. We'll go to Mars again and have a real vacation."

Alice faded away. All of it faded away.

As if from a far distance the walls of Dr. Martin's laboratory seemed to close about him and the lights slowly increased. Dr. Martin was seated beside him, his head shaking slowly. "I'm so terribly sorry, Mr. Hastings. I thought we were going to get the full and true event this time. But it often happens, as in your case, that fantasy lies upon fantasy, and it is necessary to dig through great layers of them before uncovering the truth. I think, however, that we shall not have to go much deeper to find the underlying truth for you."

Mel lay on the couch, continuing to stare at the ceiling. "Then there was no great, black ship out of space?"

"Of course not! That is one danger of these analyses, Mr. Hastings. You must not be deceived into believing that a newly discovered fantasy is the truth for which you were looking. You must come back and continue your search."

"Yes. Yes, of course." He got up slowly and was helped to the outer room by the Doctor and an attendant. The attendant gave him a glass of white, sweetish substance to drink.

"A booster-upper," laughed Dr. Martin. "It takes away the grogginess that sometimes attends such a deep sweep. We will look for you day after tomorrow."

Mel nodded and stepped out into the hall.

No great black ship.

No mysterious little robot ships with tentacles that whip out and capture a man.

No strange trio in surgeons' gowns.

And no Alice—

A sudden spear of thought pierced his mind. Maybe all that was illusion, too. Maybe he could go home right now and find her waiting for him. Maybe—

No. That was real enough. The accident. Dr. Winters. The scene in the icy room next to Surgery at the hospital. Dr. Martin didn't know about that. He would have called that a fantasy, too, if Mel had tried to tell him.

No. It was all real.

The unbelievable, alien organs of Alice.

The great, black ship.

The mindless robot searchers.

His nightmare had stemmed from all this that had happened out in space, which had somehow been wiped from his conscious memory. The nightmare had not existed in his boyhood, as he had thought. It was oriented in time now.

But what had happened to Alice? There was no clue in the memory unearthed by Dr. Martin. Was her condition merely the result of some freak heredity or gene mutation?

The surging turmoil in his mind was greater than before. There was only one way to quiet it—that was to carry out his original plan to go to Mars.

He'd go out there again. He'd find out if the black ship existed or not.

The girl in the ticket office was kind but firm. "Our records show that you were a vacationer to Mars very recently. The demand is so great and the ship capacity so small that we must limit vacation trips to no more than one in any ten-year period."

He turned away and went down the hall and out the doorway of the marble and brass Connemorra Lines Building.

He walked through town for six blocks and the thought of old Jake Norton came to his mind. Jake had been an old timer in the city room when Mel was a cub. Jake had retired just a few months ago and lived in a place in town with a lot of other old men. Mel hailed the nearest cab and drove to Jake's place.

"Mel, it's great to see you!" Jake said. "I didn't think any of the boys would remember an old man after he'd walked out for the last time."

"People remember real easy when they want favors."

"Sure," Jake said with a grin, "but there's not much of a favor I can do you any more, boy. Can't even loan you a ten until next payday."

"Jake, you can help me," said Mel. "You don't expect to ever take a trip to Mars, do you?"

"Mars! Are you crazy, Mel?"

"I went once. I've got to go again. It's about Alice. And they won't let me. I didn't know you could go only once in ten years."

Jake remembered. Alice had called him and all the other boys after they'd come back the other time. Mel had been sick, she said. He wouldn't remember the trip. They were asked not to say anything about it. Now Mel was remembering and wanted to go again. Jake didn't know what he should do.

"What can I do to help you?" he asked.

"I'll give you the money. Buy a ticket in your name. I'll go as Jake Norton. I think I can get away with it. I don't think they make any closer check than that."

"Sure—if it'll do you any good," Jake said hesitantly. He was remembering the anxiety in Alice's voice the day she called and begged him not to say anything that would remind Mel of Mars. No one ever had, as far as Jake knew.

He took the money and Mel waited at the old men's home. An hour later Jake called. "Eight months is the closest reservation I can get at normal rates, but I know of some scalpers who charge 50% more."

Mel groaned. "Buy it no matter what the cost! I've got to go at once!" He would be broke for the next ten years.

I t was little different from the other time. There was the same holiday excitement in the crowd of vacationers and those who had come to see them off. It was the same ship, even.

All that was different was the absence of Alice.

He stayed in his stateroom and didn't watch the

takeoff. He felt the faint rocking motion as the ship went down its long waterway. He felt the shift as the artificial gravity took over. He lay on the bed and closed his eyes as the Martian Princess sought the cold night of space.

For two days he remained in the room, emerging only for meals. The trip itself held no interest for him. He waited only for the announcement that the black ship had come.

But by the end of the second day it had not come. Mel spent a sleepless night staring out at the endless horizon of stars. Dr. Martin had been right, he thought. There was no black ship. He had merely substituted one illusion for another. Where was reality? Did it exist anywhere in all the world?

Yet, even if there were no black ship, his goal was still Mars.

The third day passed without the appearance of the black ship. But on the very evening of that day the speaker announced: "All passengers will prepare for transfer from the shuttle ship to the Mars liner. Bring hand luggage—"

Mel sat paralyzed while he listened to the announcement. So it was true! He felt the faint jar that rocked the Martian Princess as the two ships coupled. From his stateroom port Mel could see the stranger, black, ugly, and somehow deadly. He wished he could show Dr. Martin this "illusion"!

He packed swiftly and left the room. Mel joined the surprised and excited throng now, not hanging back, but eager to find out the secret of the great black ship.

The transition from one ship to the other was almost imperceptible. The structure of both corridors was the same, but Mel knew when the junction was crossed. He sensed the entry into a strange world that was far different from the common one he knew.

Far down the corridor the crowd was slowing, forming into lines before stewards who were checking tickets. The passengers were shunted into branching corridors leading to their own staterooms. So far everything was so utterly normal that Mel felt an overwhelming despondency. It was just as they had been told; they were transferring to the Mars liner from the shuttle.

The steward glanced at his ticket, held it for a moment of hesitation while he scanned Mel's face. "Mr. Norton—please come with me."

The steward moved away in a direction no other passengers were taking. Another steward moved up to his place. "That way," the second man said to Mel. "Follow the steward."

Mel's heart picked up its beat as he stepped out of the line and moved slowly down the corridor after the retreating steward. They walked a long way through branching silent corridors that showed no sign of life.

They stopped at last before a door that was like a score of others they had passed. There were no markings. The steward opened the door and stood aside. "In here please," he said. Mel entered and found himself alone. The steward remained outside.

The room was furnished as an office. It was carpeted and paneled luxuriously. A door leading from a room at his left opened and admitted a tall man with graying hair. The man seemed to carry an aura of power and strength as he moved. An aura that Mel Hastings recognized.

"James Connemorra!" Mel exclaimed.

The man bowed his head slightly in acknowledgement. "Yes, Mr. Hastings," he said.

Mel was dismayed. "How do you know who I am?" he said.

James Connemorra looked through the port beside Mel and at the stars beyond. "I have been looking for you long enough I ought to know who you are."

Something in the man's voice chilled Mel. "I have been easy enough to find. I'm only a news reporter. Why have you been looking for me?"

Connemorra sank into a deep chair on the opposite side of the room. "Can't you guess?" he said.

"It has something to do with what happened—before?" Mel asked. He backed warily against the opposite wall from Connemorra. "That time when I escaped from the Martian Princess rather than come aboard the black ship?"

Connemorra nodded. "Yes."

"I still don't understand. Why?"

"It's an old story." Connemorra shrugged faintly. "A man learns too much about things he should know nothing of."

"I have a right to know what happened to my wife. You know about her don't you?"

Connemorra nodded.

"What happened to her? Why was she different after her trip to Mars?"

James Connemorra was silent for so long that Mel thought he had not heard him. "Is everyone different when they get back?" Mel demanded. "Does something happen to everybody who takes the Mars trip, the same thing that happened to Alice?"

"You learned so much," said Connemorra, speaking as if to himself, "I had to hunt you down and bring you here."

"What do you mean by that? I came through my own efforts. Your office tried to stop me."

"Yet I knew who you were and that you were here. I must have had something to do with it, don't you think?"

"What?"

"I forced you to come by deception, so that no one knows you are here—except the old man whose name you used. Who will believe him that you came on the Martian Princess? Our records will show that a Jake Norton will be there on Earth. No one can ever prove that Mel Hastings ever came aboard."

Mel let his breath out slowly. His fear suddenly swallowed caution. He took a crouching step forward. Then he stopped, frozen. James Connemorra tilted the small pistol resting in his lap. Mel did not know how it came to be there. He had not seen it a moment ago.

"What are you going to do?" Mel demanded. "What are you going to do with all of us?"

"You know too much," said Connemorra, shrugging in mock helplessness. "What *can* I do with you?"

"Explain what I don't understand about the things you say I know."

"Explain to you?" The idea seemed to amuse Connemorra greatly, as if it had some utterly ridiculous aspect. "Yes, I might as well explain," he said. "I haven't had anyone interested enough to listen for a long time.

"Men have never been alone in space. We have been watched, inspected, and studied periodically since Neanderthal times by races in the galaxy who have preceded us in development by hundreds of thousands of years. These observers have been pleasantly excited by some of the things we have done, appalled by others.

"There is a galactic organization that has existed for at least a hundred thousand years. This organization exists for the purpose of mutual development of the worlds and races of the galaxy. It also exists to maintain peace, for there were ages before its organization when interstellar war took place, and more than one great world was wiped out in such senseless wars.

"When men of Earth were ready to step into space, the Galactic Council had to decide, as it had decided on so many other occasions, whether the new world was to be admitted as a member. The choice is not one which a new world is invited to make; the choice is made for it. A world which begins to send its ships through space becomes a member of the Council, or its ships cease to travel. The world itself may cease to exist."

"You mean this dictatorial Council determines whether a world is fit to survive and actually wipes out those it decides against?" gasped Mel in horror. "They set themselves up as judges in the Universe?"

"That's about the way they operate, to put it bluntly," said Connemorra. "You can call them a thousand unpleasant names, but you can't change the fact of their existence, nor the fact of their successful operation for a period as long as the age of the human race.

"They would never have made their existence known to us if we had not begun sending our ships into space. But once we did that we were entering territory staked out by races that were there when we crawled out of our caves. Who can say what their rights are?"

"But to pass judgment on entire worlds—"

"We have no choice but to accept that such judgment is passed."

"And their judgment of Earth—?"

"Was that Earth was not ready for Council membership. Earthmen are still making too many blunders to join creatures that could cross the galaxy at the speed of light when we were learning how to chip flint."

"But they didn't wipe us out!"

James Connemorra looked out at the stars. "I wonder," he said. "I wonder—"

"What do you mean?" Mel said in a tight voice.

"We have defects which are not quite like any they have encountered before. We have developed skills in the manufacture of artifacts, but we have no capacity for using them. For example, we have developed vast systems of communication, but these systems have not improved our communications they have actually blocked communication."

"That's crazy!" said Mel. "Do they suppose smoke signals are superior to the 3-d screens in our homes?"

"As a matter of fact, they do. And so do I. When a man must resort to smoke signals he is very certain that he has something to say before he goes to the trouble of putting the message in the air. But our fabulous screens prevent us from communicating with each other by throwing up a wall of pseudo-communication that we can't get through. We subject ourselves to a barrage of sound and light that has a communication content of almost zero.

"The same is true of our inventions in transportation. We have efficient means of travel to all parts of the world and now to the Universe itself. But we don't travel. We use our machines to block traveling."

"I can understand the first argument, but not this one!" said Mel.

"We move our bodies to new locations with our machines, but our minds remain at home. We take our rutted thoughts, our predispositions, our cultural concepts wherever we go. We do not touch, even with a fragment of our minds, that which our machines give us contact with. We do not travel. We move in space, but we do not travel.

"This is their accusation. And they're right. We are still doing what we have always done. We are using space flight for the boring, the trivial, the stupid; using genius for a toy, like a child banging an atomic watch on the floor. It happened with all our great discoveries and inventions: the gasoline engine, the telephone, the wireless. We've built civilizations of monumental stupidity on the wonders of nature. One race of the Galactics has a phrase they apply to people like us: 'If there is a God in Heaven He has wept for ten thousand years.'

"But all this is not the worst. A race that is merely stupid seldom gets out to space. But ours has something else they fear: destructiveness. They have plotted our history and extrapolated our future. If they let us come out, war and conflict will follow."

"They can't know that!"

"They say they can. We are in no position to argue."

"So they plan to destroy us—"

"No. They want to try an experiment that has been carried out just a few times previously. They are going to reduce us from what they term the critical mass which we have achieved."

"Critical mass? That's a nuclear term."

"Right. Meaning ready to blow up. That's where we are. Two not-so-minor nuclear wars in fifty years. They see us carrying our destructiveness into space, fighting each other there, infecting other races with our hostility. But if we are broken down into smaller groups, have the tools of war removed, and are forced to take another line of development—well, they have hopes of salvaging us."

"But they can't do a thing like that to us! What do they intend? Taking groups of Earthmen, deporting them to other worlds—breaking them apart from each other forever—?"

The coldness found its resting place in Mel's chest. He stared at James Connemorra. Then his eyes moved slowly over the walls of the room in the black ship and out to the stars. The black ship.

"This ship—! You transfer your passengers to this Galactic ship for deportation to other worlds! But they come back—"

"They are sent to colonies on other worlds where conditions are like those on Earth—with significant exceptions. The colonies are small, the largest are only a few thousand. The problems there are different than on Earth—and they are tough. The natural resources are not the same. The development of the resulting cultures will be vastly different from that of Earth. The Galactic Council is very interested in the outcome—which will not be known with certainty for a thousand years or so."

"But they come back," Mel repeated. "You bring them back!"

"For each Earthman who goes out, a replacement is sent back. The replacement is an android supplied by the Council."

"Android!" Mel felt his reason slipping. He knew he was shouting. "Then Alice—the Alice that died was an android, she was not my wife! My Alice is still alive! You can take me to her—"

Connemorra nodded. "Alice is still alive, and well. No harm has come to her."

"Take me to her!" Mel knew he was pleading, but in his anguish he had no pride.

Connemorra seemed to ignore his plea. "Earth's population is slowly being diluted by the removal of top people. The androids behave in every way like the individuals they replace, but they are preconditioned against the inherent destructiveness of Earthmen."

Blind anger seemed to rise within Mel. "You have no right to separate me from Alice. Take me to her!"

His rage ignited and he leaped forward.

The small gun in Connemorra's hand spurted twice. Mel felt a double impact in a moment of great wonder. It couldn't end like this, he thought. It couldn't end without his seeing Alice once more. Just once more—

He sank to the floor. The pain was not great, but he knew he was dying. He looked down at his hand that covered the great wound in his mid-section. There was something wrong.

He felt the stickiness, but the red blood was not welling out. Instead, a thick bubble of green ooze moved from the wound and spread over his clothes and his hand. An alien greenness that was like nothing human.

He had seen it once before.

Alice.

He stared up at Connemorra with wide, wondering eyes.

"Everything went wrong, my poor android," said Connemorra softly. "After your human was brought back to the ship we were forced to go through with the usual process of imprinting his mind content upon his android. But we had to wipe out all memory of the attempted escape from the Martian Princess. This was not successful. It still clung in the nightmares you experienced. And the psycho-recovery brought it all back.

"We tried to cover it with an amnesiac condition instead of the usual pre-printed memory of a Mars vacation. And all this might have worked if the Alice android had not been defective also. A normal android has protective mechanisms that make accidents and subsequent discovery impossible. But the Alice android failed, and you set out on a course to uncover us. I had to find a way to destroy you—murder.

"I'm truly sorry. I don't know how an android thinks or feels. Sometimes I'm afraid of all of you. You are like men, but I've seen the factories in which you are produced. There are many things I do not know. I know only that I had to obey the Galactic Council or Earth would have been destroyed long ago.

"And something else I know: Alice and Mel Hastings are content and happy. They are on a lovely world, very much like Central Valley."

He closed his eyes as he felt the life—or whatever it was—seeping out of him. It came out right, after all, he thought.

Like a wooden soldier with a painted smile, fallen from a shelf, he lay twisted upon the floor

CUBS OF THE WOLF

In the spring the cherry blossoms are heavy in the air over the campus of Solarian Institute of Science and Humanities. On a small slope that rims the park area, Cameron Wilder lay on his back squinting through the cloud of pink-white petals to the sky beyond. Beside him, Joyce Farquhar drew her jacket closer with an irritated gesture. It was still too cold to be sitting on the grass, but Cameron didn't seem to notice it—or anything else, Joyce thought.

"If you don't submit a subject for your thesis now," she said, "you'll take another full six months getting your doctorate. Sometimes I think you don't really want it!"

Cameron stirred. He shifted his squinting gaze from the sky to Joyce and finally sat up. But he was staring ahead through the trees again as he took his pipe from his pocket and began filling it slowly.

"I *don't* want it if it's not going to mean anything after I get it," he said belligerently. "I'm not going to do an investigation of some silly subject like The Transience of Venusian Immigrants in Relation to the Martian Polar Ice Cap Cycle. Solarian sociologists are the butt of enough ridicule now. Do something like that and for the rest of your life you get knocking of the knees whenever anybody inquires about the specialty you worked in and threatens to read your thesis."

"Nobody's asking you to do anything you don't want to. But *you* picked the field of sociology to work in. Now I don't see why you have to act such a purist that it takes months to find a research project for your degree. Pick something—anything!—I don't care what it is. But if you don't get a degree and an appointment out of the next session I don't think we'll ever get married—not ever."

Cameron removed his pipe from his mouth with a precise grip and considered it intently as it cupped in his hands. "I'm glad you mentioned marriage," he said. "I was just about to speak of it myself."

"Well, don't!" said Joyce. "After three years—Three years!"

He turned to face her and smiled for the first time. He liked to lead her along occasionally just to watch her explode, but he was not always sure when he had gone too far. Joyce had a mind like a snapping, random matching calculator while he operated more on a slow, carefully shaping analogue basis, knowing things were never quite what they seemed but trying to get as close an approximation of the true picture as possible.

"Will you marry me now?" he said.

The question did not seem to startle her. "No degree, no appointment—and no chance of getting one—we couldn't even get a license. I hope you aren't suggesting we try to get along without one, or on a forgery!"

Cameron shook his head. "No, darling, this is a perfectly bona fide proposal, complete with license, appointment, the works—what do you say?"

"I say this spring sun is too much for you." She touched the dark mass of his hair, warmed by the sun's rays, and put her head on his shoulder. She started to cry. "Don't tease me like that, Cameron. It seems like we've been waiting forever—and there's still forever ahead of us. You can't do anything you want to—"

Cameron put his arms about her, not caring if the whole Institute faculty leaned out the windows to watch. "That's why you should appreciate being about to marry such a resourceful fellow," he said more gently. And now he dropped all banter. "I've been thinking about how long it's been, too. That's why I decided to try to kill a couple of sparrows with one pebble."

Joyce sat up. "You aren't serious—?"

Cameron sucked on his pipe once more. "Ever hear of the Markovian Nucleus?" he said thoughtfully.

Joyce slowly nodded her head. "Oh, I think I've heard the name mentioned," she murmured, "but nothing more than that."

"I've asked for that as my research project."

"But that's clear out of the galaxy—in Transpace!"

"Yes, and obviously out of bounds for the ordinary graduate researcher. But because of the scholarship record I've been able to rack up here I took a chance on applying to the Corning Foundation for a grant. And they decided to take a chance on me after considerable and not entirely painless investigation. That's why you were followed around like a suspected Disloyalist for a month. My application included a provision for you to go along as my wife. Professor Fothergill notified me this morning that the grant had been awarded."

"Cam—" Joyce's voice was brittle now. "You aren't fooling me?"

He gathered her in his arms again. "You think I

would fool about something like that, darling? In a week you'll be Mrs. C. Wilder, and as soon as school is out, on your way to the Markovian Nucleus. And besides, it took me almost as much work preparing the research prospectus as the average guy spends on his whole project!"

S ometimes Joyce Farquhar wished Cameron were a good deal different than he was. But then he wouldn't have been Cameron, and she wouldn't want to marry him, she supposed. And somehow, while he fell behind on the mid-stretch, he always managed to come in at the end with the rest of the field. Or just a little bit ahead of it.

Or a good deal ahead of it. As now. It took her a few moments to realize the magnitude of the coup he had actually pulled off. For weeks she had been depressed because he refused to use some trivial, breeze research to get his degree. He could have started it as much as a year ago, and they could have been married now if he'd set himself up a real cinch.

But now they were getting married anyway—and Cameron was getting the kind of research deal that would satisfy his frantic desire for integrity in a world where it counted for little, and his wish to contribute something genuine to the sociological understanding of sentient creatures.

Their marriage, as was customary, would be a cut and dried affair. A call to the license bureau, receipt of formal sanction in the mail—she supposed Cameron had already made application—and a little party with a few of their closest friends on the campus. She wished she had lived in the days when getting married was much easier to do, and something to make a fuss about.

She stirred and sat up, loosening the jacket as the sun came from behind a puff of cloud. "You could have told me about this a long time ago, couldn't you?" she said accusingly.

Cameron nodded. "I could have. But I didn't want to get false hopes aroused. I didn't have much hope the deal would actually go through, myself. I think Fothergill is pretty much responsible for it."

"Transpace—" Joyce said dreamily. "Tell me about the Markovian Nucleus. Why is it important enough for a big research study, anyway?"

"It's a case of a leopard who changed his spots," said Cameron. "And nobody knows how or why. The full title of the project is A Study of the Metamorphosis of the Markovian Nucleus."

"What happened? How are they any different from the way they used to be?"

"A hundred and fifty years ago the Markovians were the meanest, nastiest, orneriest specimens in the entire Council of Galactic Associates. The groups of worlds in one corner of their galaxy, which make up the Nucleus, controlled a military force that outweighed anything the Council could possibly bring to bear against them.

"With complete disregard of any scheme of interplanetary rules or order they harassed and attacked peaceful shipping and inoffensive cultures throughout a wide territory. They were something demanding the Council's military action. But the Council lacked the strength.

"For years the Council dragged on, debating and threatening ineffectively. But nothing was ever done.

And then, so gradually it was hardly noticed, the harassments began to die down. The warlike posturing was abandoned by the Markovians. Within a period of about seventy or eighty years there was a complete about-face. They wound up as good Indians, peaceful, coöperative and intelligent members of the Council."

"Didn't anybody ever find out why?" asked Joyce.

"No. Nobody *wanted* to find out. In the early years the worlds of the Council were hiding behind their collective hands hoping with all their might that the threat might go away if they kept their eyes closed long enough. And by some miracle of all miracles, when they parted their fingers for a scared glimpse, the threat *had* disappeared.

"When they could breathe a little more easily it seemed a foolish thing to bring out this old skeleton from the closet again, so a perpetual state of hush was established. Finally, the whole thing was practically forgotten except for a short paragraph in an occasional history text. But no politician or historian has ever dared publicly to question the mysterious why of the Markovian's about-face."

"Sociologists should have done it long ago," said Joyce.

"There was always the political pressure, of course," said Cameron. "But the real reason was simply our preoccupation with making bibliographies of each others' papers. It's going to take a lot of leg work, something in which our formal courses don't give us any basic training. Fothergill understands that—it's why he pushed me so hard with the Foundation. And Riley up there is capable of seeing it, too.

"I showed him that here was a complex of at least a hundred and ten major planets, inhabited by a fairly homogenous, civilized people, speaking from a technological point of view at least. And almost overnight some force changed the entire cultural posture. I made him see that identification of that force is of no small interest to us right now. If it operated once, it could operate again—and would its results be as happy a second time?

"Riley got the Foundation to kick through enough for you and me to make a start. A preliminary survey is about all it will amount to, actually, but if we show evidence of something tangible I'll get my degree, you'll get your basic certification—and we'll both return in charge of a full-scale inquiry with a staff big enough to really dig into things next year.

"Now—about this matter of marriage which you didn't want me to speak of—"

"Keep talking, Cam—you're doing wonderfully!"

They got married at once, even though there were several weeks of school which had to be finished before they could leave. Among their friends on the campus there were a good many whispered remarks about the insanity of Joyce and Cameron in planning such a fantastic excursion, but Joyce was certain there was as much envy as criticism in the eyes of her associates. It might be true when they asserted that every conceivable sociological factor or combination of factors could be found and analyzed right here in the Solar System, but a husband who could finagle a way to combine a honeymoon trip halfway across space with his graduate research thesis was a rare specimen. Joyce played her advantage for all it was worth.

Two weeks before departure time, however, Cameron was called to the office of Professor Fothergill. As he entered he found a third man present, wearing a uniform he recognized at once as belonging to the Council Secretariat.

"I'll wait outside," he said abruptly as Fothergill turned. "I got your message and came right over. I didn't know—"

"Sit down," said Fothergill. "Cameron, this is Mr. Ebbing, whose position you no doubt recognize. Mr. Ebbing, Mr. Wilder."

The men shook hands and took seats across from each other. Fothergill sat between them at the polished table. "The Council, it seems, has developed an interest in your proposed research among the Markovians," he said. "I'll let Mr. Ebbing tell you about it."

Cameron felt a sinking anticipation within him as he turned to the secretary. Surely the Council wasn't going to actively oppose the investigation after so long a time!

The secretary coughed and shuffled the papers he drew from his case. "It's not actually the Council's interest," he said, and Cameron was immediately relieved. "But I have been asked by the Markovian Nucleus, through their representative, to suggest that they would like to save you the long and unnecessary trip. He offers to co-operate to the fullest degree by causing all necessary materials to be transferred to your site of study right here. He feels that this is the least they can do since so much interest appears to exist in the Nucleus."

Cameron stared at the secretary, trying to discern what the man's own attitude might be, but Ebbing gave no sign of playing it any way but straight.

"It sounds like a polite invitation to stay home and mind our own business," said Cameron finally. "They don't want company."

The secretary's expression changed to acknowledgment of the correct appraisal. "They don't want any investigation into the Metamorphosis of the Markovian Nucleus. There is no such thing. It is entirely a myth."

"Says the Markovians—!"

Ebbing nodded. "Says the Markovians. Other worlds, both within and without the Council have persisted in spreading tales and rumors about the Markovians for a long time. They don't like it. They are willing to co-operate in having a correct analysis of their culture published, but they don't want any more of these infamous rumors circulated."

"Then why aren't they willing to promote such an investigation? This would be their big chance—if their ridiculous position were true!"

"They *are* willing. I've told you the representative has offered to send you all needed material showing the status of their culture."

Cameron looked at the secretary for a long time before speaking again. "What's your position?" he asked finally. "Are we being ordered off the investigation?"

"The Markovian representative doesn't want to go to quite that extreme. He knows that, too, would react unfavorably towards his people. Here's his point: So far, he's blocked news of your proposed research getting to his home worlds. But he knows that if you do carry it out in the manner you propose it is going to make a lot of the home folks mighty unhappy and they'll demand to know why he didn't stop it. So he's trying to satisfy both sides at once."

"Why will the people in the Nucleus be made unhappy by our coming?"

"Because you'll go there trying to track down the basis for the rumors that defame the Markovian character. You'll bring forcibly to their attention the fact that the rest of the Universe believes the Markovians are basically a bunch of pirates."

"And the Markovians don't like to hear these things?"

"Definitely not."

"So you tell me the research is not being forbidden, but that the Markovians won't like it. Suppose I tell you, then, I'm not going to give up short of an order from the Council itself. But I am willing to camouflage the investigation if necessary. I'll make no open mention of what outside opinion says of the Markovians. I'll simply make a study of their history and character as it becomes available to me."

Ebbing nodded slowly, his eyes fixed on Cameron's face. "I would say that would be eminently satisfactory," he said. "I will inform the representative of your decision."

Then his face became more severe. "The Council will be pleased to learn of your willingness to be discreet. I wonder if you understand that the Foundation came to us upon receipt of your application, for official clearance of the project. It coincided quite fortuitously with the plans of the Council itself. For a long time we have been concerned with the lack of information regarding the Markovian situation and have been at a loss as to how to improve our situation.

"Your proposed investigation seemed the answer, but we anticipated the Markovian objection and had to make certain you would co-operate to his satisfaction. I believe this will do it."

"Why is the Council concerned?" said Cameron. "Have the Markovians changed their attitude in any way?"

"No—but the rest of us remember, even though we don't speak of it, that the Nucleus was never punished for its depredations, nor was it ever defeated. Its strength is as great as ever in proportion to the other Council worlds.

"What are the chances and potentialities of the Nucleus worlds ever again becoming the marauders they once were? That is the question which we feel must be answered. Without knowing, we are sitting on a powder keg in which the fuse may or may not be lighted. Will you bring us back the answer we need?"

Cameron felt a sudden grimness which had not been present before. "I'll do all I can," he said soberly. "If the information is there I'll bring it back."

After the secretary had gone and Fothergill turned from the door to rejoin him Cameron sat in faintly shocked consideration of the Council's unexpected support. It took his research out of the realm of the purely sociological and projected it into politics and diplomacy. He was pleased by their confidence, but not cheered by the added responsibility.

"That's a lucky break," said Fothergill enthusiastically, "and I'm beginning to suspect you may be rather badly in need of all the breaks you can get once you land among the Markovians. Don't forget for a single minute that you are dealing with the sons and grand-sons of genuine pirates."

The professor sat down again. "There's one other little item of interest I turned up the other day. You should know about it before you leave. The Markovian Nucleus is somewhat of a hotbed of Ids."

"Ids—you mean the Idealists—?"

Fothergill nodded. "Know anything about them?"

"Not much, except that they are a sort of parasitic group, living usually in a servant relationship to other races on terran-type worlds. As I recall, even they claim that they do not know the planet or even the galaxy of their origin, because they have been wan-derers for so many generations among alien races. Perhaps it would be a good idea to make a study of them, too—I don't know that a thorough one has ever been made."

"That's what I wanted to warn you about," said Fothergill, smiling. "Stick to one subject at a time. The Ids *would* make a nice research project in themselves, and maybe you can get around to it eventually. But leave them alone for the present and don't become distracted from your basic project among the Markovians. The policy of the Corning Foundation is to demand something very definite in return for the money they lay on the line. You won't get to go back next year unless you produce. That's why I don't want you to get sidetracked in any way."

II

Cameron admitted to himself that he was getting more edgy as the day of departure approached, but he tried to keep Joyce from seeing it. He was worried about the possible development of further opposition now that the Markovian had expressed his displeasure, and he was worried about their reception once they reached the Nucleus. He wondered why they had not seen in advance that it would be an obvious blunder to let the Markovians be aware of their real purpose. It didn't even require a pirate ancestry to make groups unappreciative about resurrection of their family skeletons.

But no other hindrance appeared, and on the evening before their departure Fothergill called that word had been received from Ebbing stating the Markovian representative had approved the visit now that Cameron had expressed a change in his objectives. Their coming had been announced to the Markovian people and the way prepared for an official welcome.

Cameron was pleased by the change of attitude. He was hit for the first time, however, by the full force of the fact that he was taking his bride to a pirate center which the Council had never overthrown and which was active only moments ago, culturally speaking.

If any kind of trouble should develop the Council would be almost impotent in offering them assistance. On the face of it, there was no reason to expect trouble. But the peculiarly oblique opposition of the

Markovian delegate in the Council continued to make him uneasy.

His tentative suggestion that he would feel better if he knew she were safe on Earth brought a blistering response from Joyce, which left him with no doubts about carrying out his original plans.

And then, as the last of their packing was completed and they were ready to call it a day, the phone buzzed. Cameron hesitated, determined to let it go unanswered, then punched the button irritably on audio only.

Instead of the caller, he heard the voice of the operator. "One moment please. Interstellar, Transpace, printed. Please connect visio."

It was like a shock, he thought afterwards. There was no one he knew who could be making such a call to him. But automatically he did as directed. Joyce had come up and was peering over his shoulder now. The screen fluttered for a moment with polychrome colors and cleared. The message, printed for English translation, stood out sharply. Joyce and Cameron exclaimed simultaneously at the titling. It was from Premier Jargla, Executive Head of the Markovian Government.

"To Wilder, Cameron and Joyce," it read, "greetings and appreciation for your proposed visit to the Markovian Nucleus for study of our history and customs. We have not been before so honored. We feel, however, that it is an imposition on your Foundation and on you personally to require that you make the long journey to the Nucleus for this purpose alone. While we would be honored to entertain you—"

It was the same proposition as Ebbing had reported the delegate offered. Only this time it was from the head of the Markovian government himself.

They sat up nearly all the rest of the night considering this new development. "Maybe you shouldn't go, after all," said Joyce once. "Maybe this is something that needs bigger handling than we can possibly give it."

Cameron shook his head. "*I've* got to go. They haven't closed the door and said we can't come. If I backed out before they did, I'd be known the rest of my life as the guy who was *going* to crack the Markovian problem. But I'd much rather you—"

"No! If you're going, so am I."

They consulted again with Fothergill and finally drafted as polite a reply as possible, explaining they were newly married, desired to make the trip a honeymoon excursion primarily and conduct an investigation into Markovian culture to prevent the waste of the wonderful opportunity their visit would afford them.

An hour before takeoff a polite acknowledgment came back from the Nucleus assuring them a warm welcome and congratulating them on their marriage. They went at once to the spaceport and took over their stateroom. "Before anything else happens to try to pull us off this investigation," Cameron said.

The trip would be a long one, involving more than two months subjective time, because no express runs moved any distance at all in the direction of the Nucleus. It was necessary to transfer three times, with days of waiting between ships on planets whose surface conditions permitted exploration only in cumbersome suits that could not be worn for more than short periods. Most of the waiting time was spent in the visitors' chambers at the landing fields.

These seemed to grow progressively worse. The last one could not maintain a gravity below 2G, and the minimum temperature available was 104 degrees. There was a three-day wait here and Joyce spent most of it lying on the bed, under the breeze of a fan which seemed to have required a special dispensation of the governing body to obtain.

Cameron, however, was unwilling to spend his time this way in spite of the discomfort imposed by any kind of activity. Humidity was a physical factor which seemed to have gone undiscovered by the inhabitants of the planet they were on. He was sure it was constantly maintained within a fractional per cent of one hundred as he donned a clean pair of trunks and staggered miserably along the corridor toward a window that gave a limited view of the city about them.

That was when he discovered that they were to be accompanied on the remainder of the journey by a Markovian citizen and his Id servant.

The visitors' chamber in which these semi-terran conditions were supplied consisted of only three suites. The other two had been empty when Cameron and Joyce arrived the night before. Now a Markovian Id occupied a seat by the window. He glanced up with warm friendliness and invited Cameron to join him.

Cameron hesitated, undecided for a moment whether to return to his suite for the portable semantic translator used in his profession at times like this. He always felt there was something decidedly unprofessional about resorting to their use and had spent many hours trying to master Markovian before leaving. He understood the Id well enough and decided to see if he could get along without the translator.

"Thanks," he said, taking a seat. "I don't suppose there's much else to do except look at the scenery here."

The Id showed obvious surprise that Cameron spoke the language without use of an instrument. His look of pleasure increased. "It is not often we find one of your race who has taken the trouble to make himself communicable with us. You must be expecting to make a long stay?"

Cameron's sense of caution returned as he remembered the previous results of indiscreet announcement of his purpose. He wiped the stream of sweat from his face and neck and took a good look at the Id.

The Idealists were of an anthropomorphic race, dark-skinned like the terran Indian. Very few of them had ever appeared on Earth, however, and this was actually Cameron's first view of one in the flesh. He knew something of their reputation and characteristics from very brief study at the Institute—but no one really knew very much of the Ids as far as Earthmen were concerned. The warning of Fothergill to keep to the main line of his research sank to the bottom of his mind as he leaned toward the stranger with a fresh sense of excitement inside him.

"I have never felt you could understand another man unless you spoke his language," he said in his not too stumbling Markovian.

The Id, like himself, was dressed in the briefest of

garments and perspiration poured from the dark skin as he nodded. "You speak sounder wisdom than one usually meets in a stranger," he said. "May I introduce myself: Sal Karone, servant of the Master Dalls Ret Marthasa?"

Cameron introduced himself and cautiously explained that he and Joyce were on their honeymoon, but had a side interest in the history and customs of the Markovian Nucleus. "My people know so little about you," he said, "it would be a great privilege to be able to take back information that would increase our mutual understanding."

"All that the Idealists have belongs to every man and every race," said Sal Karone solemnly. "What we can give you may be had for the asking. But I would give you a word of warning about my Masters."

Cameron felt the flesh of his back tingle with sudden chill as the eyes of the Id turned full upon him.

"Do not try to find out the hidden things of the Masters. That is what you have come for, is it not, Cameron Wilder? That is why you have taken so much trouble to learn the language which we speak. I say do not inquire of the things about which they do not wish to speak. My Masters are a people who cannot yet be understood by the men of other worlds. In time there will be understanding, but that time is not yet. You will only bring disaster and disappointment upon us and yourselves by attempting to hasten that time."

"I assure you I have no intention of prying," said Cameron haltingly. He fumbled for the right Markovian words. "You have misunderstood—We come only in friendship and with no intention of disturbing—"

The Id nodded sagely. "So many crises are originated by good intentions. But I am sure that now you understand the feelings of my Masters in these things that you will be concerned only with your own enjoyment while in the Nucleus. And do come to the centers of the Idealists, for there is much we can show you, and our willingness has no limits."

For a moment it was impossible for Cameron to remember that he was dealing with a mere servant of the Markovians. The Id's words were so incisive and his manner so commanding that it seemed he must be speaking in his own right.

And then his manner changed. His boldness vanished and he spoke obsequiously. "You will forgive me," he said, "but this is a matter concerning which there is much feeling."

Cameron Wilder was more than willing to agree with this sentiment. As he returned to his own quarters he debated telling Joyce of his encounter with the Id, deciding finally that he'd have to mention it since they'd all be traveling together, but omitting the Id's repetition of the previous warnings.

He did not meet the Markovian, nor did he encounter the Id again in the waiting quarters. It was not until they had embarked on the last leg of the journey and had been aboard the vessel for half a day that they met a second time.

The ship was not a Markovian or a terran-type vessel of any kind. Another week's wait would have been required for one of those. As it was, their quarters were not too uncomfortable although very limited. The bulk of the vessel was designed for crew and passengers very much unlike Terran or Markovian, and only a few suites were provided for accommodation of such races.

This threw the travelers to the Nucleus in close association again. Their suites opened to a common lounge deck and when Cameron and Joyce went out they found Sal Karone and the Markovian, Marthasa, already there.

The Id was on his feet instantly. With a sharp bow he introduced the newcomers to his Master. Dells Marthasa stood and extended a hand with a smile. "I believe that is your greeting on Earth, is it not?" he said.

"You must be familiar with our home world," said Cameron, returning the handshake.

"Only a little, through my studies," said the Markovian. "Enough to make me want to hear much more. Please join us. Since my *sargh* told me we would be traveling together I have looked forward to your company."

The term, *sargh*, as Cameron learned shortly was applied to all Ids attached to Markovians. It had a connotation somewhere between servant and companion. Sal Karone remained in the background, but there was no servility in his manner. His eyes remained respectfully—almost fondly; that was the right word, Cameron thought curiously—on Marthasa.

While the Id was slender in build, the Markovian was taller and bulkier. His complexion was also dark, but not quite so much so as the Id's. He was dressed in loose, highly colored attire that gave Cameron an impression of an Oriental potentate of his own world.

But somehow there was a quality in Marthasa's manner that was jarring. It would have been less so if the Markovian had been less anthropomorphic in form and feature, but Cameron found it difficult to think of him as anything but a fellow man.

A man of arrogance and ill manners, and completely unaware that he was so.

It was apparent in his gestures and in the negligence with which he leaned back and surveyed his companions. "You'll be surprised when you see the Nucleus," he said. "We sometimes hear of rumors circulated among Council worlds that Markovian culture is rather backward."

"I've never heard anything of that kind," said Cameron. "In fact we've heard almost nothing at all of the Nucleus. That's why we decided to come."

"I'm sure we can make you glad you did. Don't you think so, Karone?"

The face of the Id was very sober as he nodded solemnly and said, "Indeed, Master." His burning eyes were boring directly into Cameron's own.

"I want to hear about your people, about Earth," said Marthasa. "Tell me what you would like to see and do while you're in the Nucleus."

While Joyce answered, explaining they hardly knew what there was to be seen, Cameron's attention was fixed by the problem of the strange relationship between the two men—the two races. In the face of the Id there seemed a serenity, a dignity that the Markovian would never know. Why had the Ids failed to lift themselves out of servility to a state of independence, he wondered?

Joyce explained the story about their honeymoon trip and built their interest in Markovian culture as casual indeed. As she went on, Marthasa seemed to be struck by a sudden thought.

"I insist that you make your headquarters with me during your stay," he said. "I can see that you learn everything possible about the Nucleus while you are here. My son is a Chief Historian at our largest research library and my daughter has the post of Assistant Curator at our Museum of Science and Culture. You will never have a better opportunity to examine the culture of the Nucleus!"

Cameron winced inwardly at the thought of Marthasa's companionship during their whole stay, and yet the Markovian's statement might be perfectly true—there would be no better opportunity to make their study.

"We have an official note of welcome from your Executive Head, Premier Jargla," he said. "While we would be very happy to accept your invitation, it may be that he has different plans for our reception."

Marthasa waved a hand. "I shall arrange for my appointment as your official host. Consider it agreed upon!"

It was agreed. But Joyce was not as optimistic as Cameron in regarding it an aid to their study. "If they have a general aversion to talking about their pirate ancestry, Marthasa is just the boy to put us off the track," she said. "If he gets a clue to what we really want to know, he'll keep us busy looking at everything else until we give up and go home."

Cameron leaned back in the deep chair with his hands behind his head. "It's not too hard to imagine Marthasa's great-great-grandfather running down vessels in space and pillaging helpless cities on other planets. The veneer of civilization on him doesn't look very thick."

"It's not hard to imagine Marthasa doing it," said Joyce. "A scimitar between his teeth would be completely in character!"

"If all goes well, you will probably see just that—figuratively speaking, of course. Where a cultural shift has been so great as this one you are certain to see evidence of both levels in conflict with one another. It's like a geologic fault line. Once we learn enough about the current mores the anomalies will stand out in full view. That's what we want to watch for."

"One thing that's out of character right now is his offer of assistance through his son, the Chief Historian," said Joyce. "That doesn't check with the previous invitations to stay home. Once they let us have access to their historical records we'll have them pegged."

"We haven't got it yet," said Cameron. "We can't be sure just what they'll let us see. But for my money I'd just as soon tackle the question of the Ids. Sal Karone is twice the man Marthasa is, yet he acts like he has no will of his own when the Markovian is around."

"The Roman-slave relationship," said Joyce. "The Markovians probably conquered a large community of the Ids in their pirate days and brought them here as slaves. And I'll bet they are very much aware that the Ids are the better men. Marthasa knows it. That's why he has to put on a show in front of Sal Karone. He's the old Roman merchant struggling to keep up his conviction of superiority before the Greek scholar slave."

"The Ids aren't supposed to be slaves. According to the little that's known they are completely free. I'm

going to get Marthasa's version of it, anyway. Fothergill and the Foundation can't object to that much
investigation of the Ids."

He found the Markovian completely willing to
talk about his *sargh*. On the last day of the voyage they
managed to be alone for a time without the presence
of Sal Karone.

Marthasa shook his head in answer to Cameron's
question. "No, the *sargh* is not a slave—not in the
sense I believe you mean it. None of the Ids are. It's a
matter of religion with them to be attached to us the
way they are. They have some incomprehensible belief that their existence is of no value unless they are
serving their fellow beings. Since that means *all* of
them they can't be satisfied by serving each other so
they have to pick on some other race.

"I don't recall when they first showed up in the
Nucleus, but it's been many generations ago. There've
been Ids in my family for a half dozen generations
anyway."

"They had space flight, so they came under their
own power?" Cameron asked incredulously.

"No. Nothing like that. You can't imagine *them*
building spaceships can you? They migrated at first as
lowest-class passengers on the commercial lines. Nobody knows just where they came from. They don't
even know their home worlds. At first we tried to persuade them to go somewhere else, but then we saw
how useful they could be with their fanatic belief in
servitude.

"At present there is probably no family in the
Nucleus that doesn't have at least one Id *sargh*. Many
of us have one for every member of the family." Marthasa paused. The tone of his voice changed. "When

you've had one almost all your life as I've had Sal Karone it—well, it does something to you."

"What do you mean?" Cameron asked cautiously.

"Consider the situation from Sal Karone's point of view. He has no life whatever that is his own. His whole purpose is to give me companionship and satisfy my requirements. And I don't have to force him in any way. It's all voluntary. He's free to leave, even, any time he wants to. But I'm certain he never will."

"Why do you feel so sure of this?"

"It's hard to explain. I feel as if I've become so much a part of him that he couldn't survive alone any more. He's the one who's made it that way, not me. I have become indispensable to his existence. That's the way I explain it to myself. Most of my friends agree that this is about right."

"It's rather difficult to understand a relationship like that—unless you put it in terms I am familiar with on Earth."

"Yes—? What would it be called among your people?"

"When a man so devotes his life to another we say it is because of love."

Marthasa considered the word. "You would be wrong," he said. "It is just that in some way we have become indispensable to the Ids. They're parasites, if you want to put it that way. But they provide us a relationship we can get nowhere else, and that does us a great deal of good. That's what I meant when I said it does something to us."

"What about the Id's own culture? Haven't they any community ties among themselves, or do they ignore their own kind?"

"We've never investigated very much. I suppose

some of our scholars know the answer to that, but the rest of us don't. The Ids have communities, all right. Not all of them are in service as *sarghs* at one time. They have little groups and communities on the outskirts of our cities, but they don't amount to much. As a race they are simply inferior. They don't have the capacity for a strong culture of their own, so they can't exist independently and build a social structure like other people. It's this religion of theirs that does it. They won't let go of it, and as long as they hang onto it they can't stand on their own feet. But you don't need to feel sorry for them. We treat them all right."

"Of course—didn't mean to imply anything else," said Cameron. "Do you know if there are other Id groups serving in other galaxies?"

"Must be thousands of them altogether. Out beyond the Nucleus, away from your galaxy, you can't find a planet anywhere that isn't using the Ids. It's a wonderful setup. The Ids get what they want, and we get *sarghs* with nothing like the slave relationship you had in mind. With slaves there's rebellion, constant need of watchfulness, and no genuine companionship. A *sargh* is different. He can be a man's friend."

III

They came out of the darkness of Transpace that evening and the stars returned in the glory of a million closely gathered suns. The Markovian Nucleus lay in a galaxy of tightly packed stars that made bright the nights of all their planets. It was a spectacle for Cameron, who had traveled but little away from the Solar System, and for Joyce who had never traveled at all.

Marthasa and Sal Karone were with them in the lounge watching the screens as the ship changed drives. The Markovian squinted a moment and pointed to a minor dot near the corner of the view. "That's our destination. Another six hours and you can set foot on the best planet in the whole Universe!"

If it had been mere enthusiasm, Cameron could have taken it with tolerant understanding. But Marthasa's smugness and arrogance had not deserted him once since the beginning of this leg of the trip. Objectively, as a cultural facet to be examined, it was interesting, but Cameron agreed with Joyce that it was going to be difficult to live with.

The unsolved puzzle, however, was Sal Karone. It was obvious that the Id was sensitive to the gauche ways of the Master, yet his equally obvious devotion was unwavering.

Marthasa had sent word ahead to the government that he desired the Terrans to be his guests. Evidently he was a person of influence for assent was returned immediately.

His planet was a colorful world, banded by huge, golden deserts and pinkish seas. The dense vegetation of the habitable areas was blue with only a scattered touch of green. Cameron wondered about the chemistry involved.

The landing was made at a port that bordered a sea. The four of them were the only ones disembarking, and before the car that met them had reached the edge of the city the ship was gone again.

A pirates' lair, Cameron thought, without the slightest touch of amusement. The field looked very old, and from it he could imagine raiders had once taken off to harass distant shipping and do wanton destruction of cities and peoples on innocent worlds.

He watched the face of Marthasa as they rode through the city. There was a kind of Roman splendor in what they saw, and there was a crude Roman pride in the Markovian who was their host. The arrogance, that was not far from cruelty, could take such pride in the sweep of spaceships embarking on missions of murder and plunder.

And yet all this barbarism had been put aside. Only the arrogance remained, expressed in Marthasa's tone as he called their attention to the features of the city and landscape through which they passed. It wasn't pleasing particularly to Terran tastes, but Cameron guessed that it represented a considerable accomplishment to the Markovians. Stone appeared to be the chief building material, and, while the craftsmanship was exact, the lines of the structures lacked the grace of the Greek and Roman monuments of which Cameron was reminded.

They came at last to the house of Marthasa. There was no doubt now that he was a man of wealth or importance—probably both. He occupied a vast, villa-like structure set on a low hill overlooking the city. It was a place of obvious luxury in the economic scale of the Markovians.

They were assigned spacious quarters overlooking a garden of incredible colors beyond the transparent wall facing it. Sal Karone was also assigned duties as their personal attendant, which Cameron grasped intuitively was a gesture of supreme honor among the Markovians. He thanked Marthasa profusely for this courtesy.

After getting unpacked they were shown through the house and grounds and met Marthasa's family. His wife was a woman of considerable beauty even by Terran standards, but there was a sharpness in her manner and a sense of coldness in the small black eyes that repelled Cameron and Joyce even as the thoughtless actions of Marthasa had done.

Cameron looked carefully for the same qualities in the three smaller children who were at home, and found them easily. In none of them was there the aura of serenity possessed by the Id servants.

When they were finally alone that night Cameron sat down to make some notes on their observations up to date. "The fault line I mentioned is so obvious you can't miss it," he said to Joyce. "It's as if they're living one kind of life because they think it's the thing to do, but all their thoughts and feelings are being drawn invisibly in another direction—and they're half ashamed of it."

"Maybe the Ids have something to do with it. Remember Marthasa's statement that the relationship of the *sarghs* does something to the Markovians? If we found out exactly what that something is, we might have the answer."

Cameron shook his head. "I've tried to fit it together that way, too, but it just doesn't add up. The basic premise of the Ids is asceticism and there never was any strength in that idea. Marthasa is probably right in his estimate of the Ids. They have achieved an internal serenity but only through compensating their basic weakness with the crude strength of the Markovians and other races to which they cling. They haven't the strength to build a civilization of their own. Certainly they haven't got the power to influence the whole Nucleus. No—we'll have to look a good deal farther than the Ids before we find the answer. I'm convinced of that, even though I'd like to find out exactly what makes *them* tick. Maybe next trip—"

The following days were spent in almost profitless activity as far as their basic purpose in being in the Nucleus was concerned. Marthasa and his wife took them on long tours through the city and into the scenic areas of the continent. They promised trips over the whole planet and to other worlds of the Nucleus. There seemed no end to the sight-seeing that was proposed for them to do.

Cameron improved his facility with the language, and Joyce was beginning to get along without the translator. They were introduced to a considerable number of other Markovians, including the official representative of Premier Jargla. This gave them added contact with the Markovian character, but Marthasa and his family seemed so typical of the race that scarcely anything new was learned from the others.

At no time was anything hinted in reference to the original reluctance to have the Terrans visit the Nucleus. All possible courtesy was shown them now, and Cameron dared not mention the invitations to stay home. He felt the situation was as penetrable as a thick wall of sponge rubber backed by a ten-foot foundation of steel.

After three weeks of this, however, he cautiously broached the subject of meeting the son and daughter of Marthasa in regard to visiting the library and museum. He had met each of them just once and found them rather cool to his presence. He had not dared express his interest in their specialties at that time.

Marthasa was favorable and apologetic, however. "I have intended to arrange it," he said. "There have been so many other things to do that I have neglected your interest in these things. We won't neglect it any longer. Suppose we make an appointment for this afternoon? Zlenon will be able to give you his personal attention."

Zlenon was Marthasa's son, who held the position of Chief Historian at the research library. He was more slender and darker than his father, and lacking in his volubility and glad-handedness.

He greeted Cameron's request with a tolerant smile. "You have to be quite specific, Mr. Wilder, when you say you would like to know about the history of the Markovian Nucleus. You understand the Nucleus consists of over a hundred worlds and has a composite history extending back more than thirty thousand of your years in very minute detail."

Cameron countered with a helpless shrug and smile. "I'm afraid I'll have to depend on your good nature to guide me through such a mass. I don't intend to become a student of Markovian history, of course, but perhaps you have adequate summaries with which a stranger could start. Going backward, let us say, for perhaps two or three hundred Terran years?"

"Of course—some very excellent ones are available—" He moved toward the reading table nearby and began punching a selection of buttons.

As Cameron and Joyce moved to follow, Marthasa

waved a hand expansively and started out the other way. "I can see you're going to be set for a while. I'll just leave you here, and send the car back after I reach the house. Don't be late for dinner."

They nodded and smiled and turned to Zlenon. The Markovian was watching them with pin-point eyes. "I wondered if there was any *particular* problem in which you might be interested," he said calmly. "If there is—?"

Cameron shook his head hastily. "No—certainly not. Just general information—"

The Historian turned his attention to the table and began explaining its use to the Terrans, showing how they could obtain recording of any specific material they wished to choose. It would appear in either printed or pictorial form or could be had on audio if they wanted it. Once he was certain they could make their own selections he left them to their study.

"This is the best break we could possibly have hoped for," Joyce whispered as Zlenon disappeared from their sight. "We can get anything we want in the whole library if I understand the operation of this gadget the way I think I do."

"That's the way it looks to me," Cameron answered. "But don't get your hopes too high. There must be a catch in it somewhere, the way they were trying to shoo us away from coming here."

They punched the buttons for the history of the planet they were on, scanning slowly from the present to earlier years. There were endless accountings of trading and commercial treaties between members of the Nucleus as shifts of economic balance occurred. There were stories of explorations and benevolent contacts with races on the outer worlds. Details of their most outstanding scientific discoveries, which seemed to come with profligate rapidity—

Cameron whipped back through the pages of the histories, searching only for a single item, one clue to the swift evolution from barbarism to peaceful cooperation. After an hour he was in the middle of that critical period when the Council despaired of its inability to cope with the Markovian menace.

But the stories of commerce and invention and far-flung exchange with other peoples continued. Nowhere was there any reference to the violence of the period. They went back two hundred—five hundred years—beyond the time when Council members first made contact with the Nucleus.

There was nothing.

Cameron sat back in complete puzzlement as it became apparent that it was useless to go back further. "The normal thing would be for them to brag all over the place about their great conquests. Even races who become comparatively civilized citizens ordinarily let themselves go when it comes to history. If they've had a long record of conquest and bloodshed, they say so with plenty of chest pounding. Of course, it's padded out to reflect their righteous conquest over tyranny, but it's always there in *some* form.

"But nothing up to now has been normal about the development of the Markovian problem and this really tops it off—the complete omission of any reference to their armed conquests."

"Maybe this planet didn't participate very much. Perhaps only a small number of the Nucleus worlds were responsible for it," said Joyce.

Cameron shook his head. "No. The Council records show that the Nucleus as a unit was responsible, and that virtually all the worlds are specifically mentioned. And even if this one had been out of it completely you could still expect references to it because there was constant interchange with most of the other planets. We can try another one, though—"

They tried one more, then a half dozen in quick scanning. They swept through a summarization of the Nucleus as a whole during that critical period.

There was nothing to show that the Markovians had ever been anything but peace-loving citizens intent on pursuit of science, commerce, and the arts.

"This could have been rigged for our special benefit," said Joyce thoughtfully as they ended the day's futile search. "They didn't want to apply enough pressure to keep us from coming, but they did want to make sure we wouldn't find out anything about their past."

Cameron shook his head slowly. "It couldn't have been done in the time they've had. Simply cutting out what they didn't want to show us wouldn't have done it. There's too much cross reference to all periods involved. It's a complete phony, but it's not something done on the spur of the moment just for our benefit. It's too good for that."

"Maybe they've had it for a *long* time—just in case somebody like us should come along."

"It's possible, but I don't think that's right either," said Cameron. "I can't give you any reason for thinking so—except the phoniness goes deeper than merely deceiving an investigator. Somehow I have the feeling that the Markovians are even deceiving themselves!"

*****

They left the building and took the car back to the house of Marthasa without seeing Zlenon again. Their Markovian host was waiting. Cameron thought he sensed a trace of tension in Marthasa that wasn't there before as he led them to seats in the garden.

"We don't like to boast about the Nucleus," he said with his customary volubility, "but we have to admit we are proud of our science and technology. Few civilizations in the Universe can match it. That's not to disparage the fine accomplishments of the Terrans, you understand, but it's only *natural* that out here on these older worlds—"

They listened half attentively, trying in their imaginations to pierce the armor he used to defend so frantically the thing the Markovians did not want the outer worlds to know anything about.

The talk went on during mealtime. Marthasa's wife caught the spirit of it and they both regaled the Terrans with accounts of the grandeur of Markovian exploits. Cameron grew more and more depressed by it, and as they retired to their rooms early he began to realize how absolutely complete was the impasse into which they had been driven.

"They've let us in," he said to Joyce. "They've shown us the history they've written of themselves. There's no way in the Universe we can stand up and boldly challenge that history and call them the liars we know they are."

"But they must know of the histories written on other Council worlds about their doings," said Joyce. "Maybe we could reach a point where we could at least ask about them. Ask how it is that other histories show that a hundred and twenty years ago a fleet of Markovian ships swept unexpectedly out of space and looted and decimated the planet Lakcaine VI. Ask why the Markovian history says only that the Nucleus concluded six new commercial treaties to the benefit of all worlds concerned in that period, without any mention of Lakcaine VI."

"When you start asking questions like that you've got to be ready to run. And if it fizzles out you've lost all chance of coming back for a second try. That could fizzle out because they simply deny the validity of all history outside their own."

"Then we might as well pack and go home if you're not going to challenge any of this stuff they hand out. We won't find the answer by standing around and taking *their* word on everything."

"I forgot to tell you one thing," Cameron said slowly. "We may not have to take their word for it. Someone else here knows the truth of the situation, also."

"Who?"

"The Ids." He told her then of the warning Sal Karone had given him aboard the ship on the way to the Nucleus, the statement that "My Masters are a people who cannot yet be understood by the men of other worlds."

"The Ids know what the Markovians are and what they are trying to hide. I had almost overlooked that simple fact."

"But you can't go out and challenge them to tell the truth any more than you can the Markovians!" Joyce protested. "Because Sal Karone went out of his way to warn you doesn't mean he's going to get real buddy-buddy and tell you everything you want to know."

"No, of course not. But there's one little difference between him and the Markovians. He has admitted openly that he knows why we're here. None of the Markovians have done that yet. We don't have to challenge him because there already exists the tacit understanding that something is decidedly phony.

"And besides, he invited us to come and visit the Id communities outside the city. I think that's an invitation we should accept just as soon as possible."

IV

Sal Karone had not repeated his invitation that the Terrans visit the Id communities, but he showed no adverse reaction when Cameron said they would like to take him up on his previous offer.

"You will be very welcome," he said. A soft smile lightened his features. "I will notify my leaders you will come."

With a start, Cameron realized that the existence of any kind of community probably implied leaders, but he had ignored this in view of Marthasa's insistence that the Ids had no culture of their own. He wondered just how untrue that assertion might be.

For the first time, he sensed genuine disapproval in the attitude of Marthasa when he mentioned plans to go with Sal Karone to the Id centers. "There's nothing out there you'd want to see," the Markovian said. "Their village is only a group of crude huts in the forest. It'll be a waste of your time to go out there when there's so much else we could show you."

"Sal Karone suggested the visit before we arrived,"

said Cameron. "He'd be hurt if we turned him down. Perhaps just to satisfy him—"

Angry indecision hid behind Marthasa's eyes. "Well—maybe that makes it different," he said finally. "We try to do everything possible to make the Ids happy. It's up to you if you want to waste your time on the visit."

"I think I do. Sal Karone has been very attentive and pleasant to us. It's a small favor in return."

E arly in the morning, two days later, they left with Sal Karone directing them to the Idealist center. They discovered that the term, at the edge of the city, was a mere euphemism. It was a long two-hour trip at the high speed of which the Markovian cars were capable.

The city itself vanished, and a thickly wooded area took its place during the last half of the journey, reminding them of the few remote, peaceful forests of Earth. Then, as the car slowed, they left the highway for a rough trail that led for a number of miles back into the forest. They came at last into a clearing circled by rough wooden dwellings possessing all the appearance of crude, primitive existence on little more than a subsistence level.

"This is the village of our Chief," said Sal Karone. "He will be pleased to explain all you may wish to know about the Idealist Way."

Cameron was shocked almost beyond speech by his first sight of the clearing. He had tried to prepare for the worst, but he had told himself that the Markovian's estimate of the Ids could not be true. Now he was forced to admit that it was. In contact with all the skills of their Masters, which they would certainly be permitted to learn if they wanted to, the Ids chose primitive squalor when they were on their own.

Their serenity could be little more than the serenity of the savage who has no wants or goals and is content to merely serve those whose ambitions are greater. It was the serenity and peacefulness of death. The Ids had died—as a race—long ago. The Markovians were loud, boastful, and obnoxious, but that could be discounted as the awkwardness of youth in a race that would perhaps be very great in the Universe at a time when the Ids were wholly forgotten.

Cameron felt depressed by the sight. He began to doubt the wisdom of his coming here in hope of finding an answer to the Markovian deception. The warning of Sal Karone on shipboard seemed now like nothing more than a half ignorant demonstration of loyalty toward the Markovian Masters. Possibly there had been some talk which the Id had overheard and he had taken it upon himself to warn the Terrans— knowing perhaps nothing of the matter which the Markovians were reluctant to expose.

If he could have done so gracefully, Cameron felt he would have turned and gone back without bothering with the interview. His curiosity about the Ids themselves had all but vanished. The answer to their situation was obvious. And he had maintained such high hope that somehow his expectation in them would be fulfilled during this visit.

There was a satisfying cleanliness apparent in everything as Sal Karone led them to the largest of the buildings. Joyce seemed to be enjoying herself as she surveyed the surroundings with an interest Cameron had lost.

As they entered the doorway a thin, straight old man with a white beard arose from a chair and approached them in greeting. The ancient, conventional, patriarchal order, Cameron thought. He could see the whole setup in a nutshell right now. Squalid communities like this where the too-old and the too-young were nurtured on the calcified traditions to which nothing was ever added. The able serving in the homes of the Markovians, providing sustenance for themselves and those who depended on them. The Markovians were generous indeed in not referring to the Ids as slaves. There was little else they could ever be called.

The Chief was addressed as Venor by Sal Karone, who introduced them. "It is kind of you to include our village in your visit to the Nucleus," said Venor. "There are many more spectacular things to see."

"There is often greatest wisdom in the least spectacular," said Cameron, trying to sound like a sage. "Sal Karone was kind enough to invite us to your center and said there was much you could show us."

"The things of the soul are not possible to *show*," said Venor gently. "We wish there were time that we might teach you some of the great things our people have learned in their long wanderings. I am told that your profession and your purpose in being here is the study of races and their actions and the things they have learned."

With a start, Cameron came to greater attention. He was certain he had never given any such information in the presence of Sal Karone or Marthasa. Yet even Venor knew he was a sociologist! Here was the first knowledge that must lie behind the evidence of the undercurrent of objections of the Markovian representative in the Council and Premier Jargla.

And this primitive patriarch was in possession of it.

Relations between the individuals of this planet were something far more complex than Cameron had assumed. He hesitated a moment before speaking. Just why had this bait been so innocently thrown to him? Marthasa had never mentioned it. Yet had the Markovians asked for an attempt to get an admission from him for their own purposes? And what purposes—?

He abandoned caution, and nodded. "Yes, that is the thing I am interested in. I had hoped to study the history and ways of the Markovians. As Sal Karone has told me, they don't want strangers to make such a study. You are perhaps not so unwilling to be known—?"

"We wish the entire Universe might know of us and be as we are."

"You hardly make that possible, subjugating your identity so completely to that of another race. The worlds will never know of you unless you become strong and unified as a people and obtain a name of your own."

"Our name is known," said Venor. "We are the Idealists. You will not find many worlds on which we are unknown, and they call us the ones who serve. Even on your world you have the saying of a philosopher who taught that any who would be master should become the servant of all. Your people once understood it."

"Not as a literal undertaking," said Cameron. "You can't submerge your entire racial identity as you have done. That is not what the saying meant."

"To us it does," said Venor solemnly. "We would master the Universe—and therefore we must serve it. That is the core of the law of the Idealists."

Cameron let his gaze scan through the window to the small clearing in the thick forest, to the circle of wooden houses. *We would master the Universe*—he restrained a smile.

"You cannot believe this," said Venor, "because you have never understood the mark of the servant or the mark of the master. How often is there difficulty in distinguishing one from the other!"

And how often do the illusions of the mind ease the privations of the body, Cameron thought. So that was the source of the Idealist serenity. Wherever they went they considered themselves the masters through service—and conversely, those they served became the slaves, he supposed. It was a pleasant, easy philosophy that hurt no one. Except the ones who believed it. They died the moment they accepted it, for all initiative and desire were gone.

"The master is he who guides the destiny of a man or a race," said Venor almost in meditation. "He is not the man who gathers or disperses the wealth, or who builds the cities and the ships to the stars. The master is he who teaches what must be done with these things and how a people shall expend their lives."

"And the Markovians do this, in obedience to you?" said Cameron whimsically.

"Wherever my people are," answered Venor, "strife ceases and peace comes. Who can do this is master of worlds."

There was a strange solemnity about the voice and figure of the old Idealist that checked the sense of ridiculousness in Cameron. It seemed somehow strangely moving.

"You believe the worlds are better," he asked gently, "just because you are there?"

"Yes," said Venor, "because we are there."

There was a pathos about it that fired Cameron's anger. On scores of worlds there were primitive groups like this one, blinding themselves with a glory that didn't exist, in the grip of ancient, meaningless traditions. The younger ones—like Sal Karone—were intelligent, worth salvaging, but they could never be lifted out of this mire of false belief unless they could be shown how empty it was.

"Nothing you have said explains the mystery of how this great thing is accomplished," said Cameron almost angrily. "Even if we wanted to believe it were true, it is still as utterly incomprehensible as before we came."

"There is a saying among us," said Venor kindly. "Translated into your tongue it would be: How was the wild dog tamed, and a saddle put upon the fierce stallion?"

S tubbornly, then, Venor would say no more about the philosophy of the Idealists. He spoke freely of the many other worlds upon which the Idealists lived and served, and he affirmed the tradition that they did not even know the place of their origin, the planet that might have been their home world.

He was evasive, however, when Cameron asked when the first contact was made between his people and the Markovians. There was something that the Ids, too, were holding back, the sociologist thought, and there was no apparent reason for it.

Recklessly, he decided nothing could be lost by attempting to blast for it. "Why have the Markovians consistently lied to us?" he said. "They've given us their history—and if your people know the feelings of other worlds they know this history is a lie. Only a few generations ago the Markovians pirated and plundered these worlds, and now they pose as little tin gods with a silver halo. Why?"

Sal Karone stood by with a look of horror on his face, but Venor made no sign of alarm at this forbidden question. He merely inclined his held slowly and repeated, "How was the wild dog tamed, and a saddle put upon the fierce stallion?"

That was the end of the interview. The Ids insisted, however, that he inspect the rest of the village and they personally guided the Terrans on the tour. Cameron's trained eye took in at a glance, however, the evidence supporting his previous conclusion. The artifacts and buildings demonstrated a primitive forest culture. The other individuals he saw were almost entirely the old and very young—the ones unsuitable as servants to the Markovians. Venor explained that family life among them paralleled in general that of the Masters. Whole Idealist families lived and served as units in the Markovian household. Exceptions existed in the case of Sal Karone and others of his age who were separated from their families and had not yet begun their own.

As they returned to the car Venor took their hands. He pressed Cameron's warmly and looked into his eyes with deep sincerity. "You have made us glad by your presence," he said. "And when the time comes for you to return, we shall repay all the pleasure you have given us."

"I'm afraid we won't be able to do that," said Cameron. "We appreciate your hospitality, but I'm sure time will not permit us to visit you again, as much as we'd like to." In the past few minutes he had reached the conclusion that further research on this whole planet was futile. The best thing they could do was go somewhere else in the Nucleus and make a fresh start.

Venor shook his head, smiling. "We will see each other again, Joyce and Cameron. I feel that the day will be very soon."

It was senseless to let himself be irritated by the senile patriarch who spoke out of a world of illusion but Cameron could not help feeling nettled as he started back to the city. Somehow it seemed impossible to regard Venor as merely a specimen for sociological research. The Chief of the Idealists reached out of his unreal world and made his contact with the Terrans a personal thing—almost as if he had spent all his life waiting for their coming. There was a sense of intimacy against which Cameron rebelled, and yet it was not an unpleasant thing.

Cameron's mind oscillated between the annoyance of Venor's calm assertion that they would be back shortly, and the nonsense of the Id belief that they controlled the civilizations in which they were servants. How was the wild dog tamed, and a saddle put upon the fierce stallion?

He smiled faintly to himself, wondering if the Markovians were fully aware that the Ids regarded them as tamed dogs and saddled stallions. They couldn't help knowing, of course, but it was hard to imagine Marthasa and his wife being very much amused by such an estimate. The situation would be intolerable, however, if it were met by anything except amusement. It might be a mildly explosive subject, but he was going to find out about that one small item before moving on, anyway, Cameron decided.

S al Karone was strangely silent during the whole of the return trip. He offered no comments and made only brief, noncommittal replies to questions about the country through which they passed. He seemed depressed by the results of their visit. Probably because the violation of his warning to not question the lives of the Markovians. It was a curious evidence of their completely unreal, proprietary attitude in respect to their Masters. They'd have to investigate Marthasa's response as thoroughly as possible. There seemed to be no taboo on discussion of the Ids with him.

His annoyance at their acceptance of the invitation to the Id village appeared to have vanished as he greeted them upon their return. "We delayed eating, thinking you'd be back in time. If you'll join us in the dining room as soon as you're ready—?"

The villa of Marthasa seemed different after the day's experience with the Ids, although Cameron was certain nothing had changed either in a physical way or in their relations with the Markovians. It was as if his senses had been somehow sharpened to detect an undercurrent of feeling of which he had previously been unaware. Glancing at Joyce, he sensed she felt the same.

"I have the feeling that we missed something," she said, as they changed clothes to join Marthasa and his wife. "There was something Venor wanted us to know and wouldn't say. I would almost like to go back there again before we go away."

Cameron was surprised at his own annoyance with Joyce's statement. It reflected the impressions in his own mind which he was trying to ignore. "Nonsense," he said. "There's no use trying to read great profundity in the words of an old patriarch of the woods. He's nothing except what he appears to be."

The Markovians talked easily of Venor and the rest of the Ids. "We have tried to get him to join us in the city," said Marthasa as the meal began, "but he won't hear of it. It seems to give him a sense of importance to live out there alone with his retinue and have the other Ids come to him with their problems. He's a kind of arbiter and patriarch to all of them for many miles around."

While Marthasa talked Cameron tried to bring his awareness of all the varied facets of the problem together and see it whole, as he now understood it. The Markovians, a vast pirate community, had voluntarily abandoned freebooting for reasons yet to be discovered. They had turned their backs upon it so forcibly that they hid even the history of their depredations. And one of their last acts must have been the capture of a large colony of Idealists who were forced into servitude. Now the Ids compensated their enslavement by the religious belief that service made them masters over the ex-pirates, convincing themselves that *they* had changed the Markovians, taming them like wild dogs, saddling them as fierce stallions—

Cameron wondered if he dared, and then dismissed the thought that there could be any risk. It was too ridiculous!

There was even a half-malicious smile on his lips as he broke into Marthasa's conversation. "One of the things that made me very curious today," he said, "was the general reaction of your people to the Idealist illusion that they have *tamed* you—as expressed in their aphorism about how was the wild dog—?"

He never finished. Across the table the faces of the Markovians had frozen in sudden bitterness. The shield of friendliness vanished under the cold glare from their eyes.

Marthasa's lips seemed to curl as he whispered, "So you came like all the rest! And we wanted so much to believe you were honest. A study! A chance to find material for lies about the Nucleus to spread among all the Council worlds."

He continued almost sadly, "You will be confined to your quarters until transfer authorities can arrange for your return to Earth. And you may be sure that never again will such a scheme get one of your kind into the Nucleus again."

But there was no hint of sadness in his wife's face. She glared coldly. "I said they should never had been permitted to come!"

Cameron rose in sudden bewildered protest. "I assure you we have no intention—" he began.

And then he stopped. In one moment of incredible clarity while they stood there, eyes locked in bitter stares, he understood. He knew the myth was not a myth. It was cold, unbelievable reality. The Ids *had* tamed the Markovians.

In a moment of fear he wondered if it were anything more than a thin shell that could be shattered by a whisper from a stupid dabbler in cultures, who really knew nothing at all about the profession to which he pretended.

V

As if upon some secret signal Sal Karone appeared from the serving room at their left.

"Our visitors are no longer our guests," Marthasa said sharply with accusing eyes still upon Cameron. "They will remain in their rooms until time for deportation.

"I trust it will not be necessary to use force," he said directly to Cameron.

"Of course not. But won't you let me explain— won't you even allow an apology for breaking a taboo we did not understand?"

"Is it not taboo among all civilized peoples, including your own, to invent and spread lies about those who wish you only well?"

It was useless to argue, Cameron saw. He turned, taking Joyce's arm, and allowed Sal Karone to lead them back to their rooms. As they paused at the doorway the Id spoke without expression on his dark face.

"This is not a good thing, Cameron Wilder. It would have been best for you to have considered my warning."

He turned and stepped away, locking the door behind him.

Joyce slumped on the bed in dejection. "This is a fine fix we've got ourselves into, being declared *persona non grata* before we even get a good start! They'll remember *that* back home when A Study of the Metamorphosis of the Markovian Nucleus is mentioned in professional circles!"

"Don't rub it in," Cameron said, half angrily. "How was I to know that was such a vicious taboo? It can't be any secret to the Markovians that the Ids look upon them as tamed. Why should they get their hackles up because *I* mentioned it?"

"All I know is we're washed up as of now. What do we do when we get back home?"

Cameron stood with his back to her, looking through the windows to the garden beyond. "I'm not thinking of that," he said. "Can't you see we haven't failed? We've almost got it—the thing we came to find. We *knew* why the Markovians suddenly became good Indians. The Ids actually did tame them. We've got to find out how such an apparently impossible thing could be done."

"Do you really believe that's what happened?" asked Joyce.

Cameron nodded. "It's the only thing there is to believe. If it weren't true, Marthasa and his wife would have laughed it off as nonsense. Getting all huffy and talking about deportation for cooking up lies is the best proof you could ask for that we hit pay dirt. Don't ask me how I think the Ids could do it.

That's what I'm going to find out."

"How?"

"I don't know."

But he did have an idea that if he could somehow get word to the old Id chieftain help could be had. He knew he was straining to believe things he wanted to believe, yet it seemed as if this were almost the very thing Venor had tried to convey the day before but had left unspoken.

There was only one possibility of establishing contact, however, and that was through Sal Karone. A remote chance indeed, Cameron thought, in view of the relationship between the Markovian and his *sargh*. As a last resort it was worth trying, however.

It looked as if they would not have even this chance as the evening grew darker. Cameron kept watch through the windows in the hope of signaling Sal Karone in case he should appear. They hoped he might come to the room for a final check of their needs for the night as he usually did.

But he did not appear.

Cameron finally went to bed after Joyce was long asleep. He turned restlessly, beating his mind with increasing wonder as to how it could be so incredibly true that the Idealists were the actual masters of the Nucleus. That they had somehow tamed the murderous, piratical Markovians. He couldn't have known this was it!

One thing he could understood, however, was the Markovians reluctance to have visitors—and their careful watch over them. Marthasa had been more than a host, he thought. He was a guard as well, trying to keep the Terrans from discovering the unpleasant reality concerning the influence of the Ids. He had slipped in allowing the visit to Venor.

At dawn there was the sound of their door opening and Cameron whirled from his dressing, hopeful it might be Sal Karone. It was Marthasa, however, grim and distant. "I have obtained word that your deportation can be accomplished today. Premier Jargla has been informed and concurs. The Council has been notified and offers no protestations. You will ready yourselves before the evening hour."

He slammed the door behind him. Joyce turned down the covers in the other room and sat up. "I wonder if he isn't even going to feed us today?"

Cameron made no answer. He finished dressing hurriedly and kept a frantic watch for any sign of Sal Karone.

At last there was a knock on the door and the Id appeared with breakfast on a cart. Cameron exhaled with relief that it was not one of the other *sarghs* in the household.

Sal Karone eyed them impassively as he wheeled in and arranged the food on the table by a window. Cameron watched, estimating his chances.

"Your Chief, Venor, was very kind to us yesterday," he said quietly. "Our biggest regret in leaving is that our conversation with him must go unfinished."

Sal Karone paused. "Were there things you had yet to say to him?" he asked.

"No—there were things Venor wanted to tell us. You heard him. He wanted us to come back. It is completely impossible for us to see him again before we go?"

Sal Karone straightened and set the utensils on the table. "No, it is not impossible. I have been instructed to bring you back to the village if it should be your request."

Cameron felt a surge of eager excitement within him. "When? Our deportation is scheduled for today. How can we get there? How can we avoid Marthasa and the Markovians?"

"Stand very quietly," said Sal Karone, that sense of power and command in his voice and bearing as Cameron had seen it once before aboard the spaceship. "Now," he said. "Close your eyes."

There was a sudden wrenching twist as if two solid surfaces had slammed them from front and back, and a third force had thrust them sideways.

They opened their eyes in the wooden house of Venor, in the village of the Idealists.

"We owe you apologies," said Venor. "We hope you are not harmed in any way."

Cameron stared around uncertainly. Joyce clutched his hand. "How did we—?" Cameron stammered.

"Teleportation is the descriptive term in your language, I believe," said Venor. "It was rather urgent that you come without further delay so we resorted to it. Nothing else would do in the face of Marthasa's action. Sit down if you will, please. If you wish to rest or eat, your quarters are ready."

"Our quarters—! Then you *did* expect us back. You knew this was going to happen exactly as it has!"

"Yes, I knew," said Venor quietly. "I planned it this way when word first came to us of your visit."

"I think we are entitled to explanations," Cameron said at last. "We seem to have been pieces in a game we knew nothing about."

And it had taken this long for the full impact of Venor's admission of teleportation to hit him. He closed his eyes in a moment's reaction of fright. He didn't want to believe it—and knew he must. These Idealists—who could master galaxies and tame the wild Markovians—was there anything they could not do?

"Not a game," Venor protested. "We planned this because we wanted you to see what you have seen. We wanted a man of Earth to know what we have done."

"But don't the Markovians realize the foolishness of deporting us because we stumbled onto the relationship between you and them? And if you are in control how can they issue such an order—unless you want it?"

"Our relationship is more complex than that. There are different levels of control. We operate the one that brought you here—" He let Cameron consider the implication of the unfinished statement.

Then he continued, "To understand the Markovians' reason for deporting you, consider that on Earth men have tamed wolves and made faithful, loyal dogs who can be trusted. Dogs who have forever lost the knowledge their ancestors were fierce marauders ready to rip and tear the flesh of any man or beast that came their way.

"Consider the dogs only a generation or two from the vicious wolves who were their forebears. The old urges have not entirely died, yet they want to know man's affection and trust. Could you remind them of what their kind once was without stirring up torment within them?

"So it is with the Markovians. They are peaceful

and creative, but only a few generations behind them are pirates who were not fit to sit in the Councils of civilized beings. They have no tradition of culture to support them. It knocks the props out from under them, so to speak, to have it known what lies behind them. They cannot be friends with such a man. They cannot even endure the knowledge among themselves."

"Then I was right!" Cameron exclaimed. "Their phony history *was* set up to deceive their own people as well as others."

"Yes. The dog would destroy all evidence of his wolf ancestry. It has been an enormous project, but the people of the Nucleus have been at it a long time. They have concocted a consistent history which leaves out all evidence of their predatory ancestry. The items of reality which were possible to leave have been retained. The gaps between have been bridged by fictionized accounts of glorious undertakings and discoveries. Most of the Markovian science has been taken from other cultures, but now their history boasts of heroes and discoverers who never lived and who were responsible for all the great science they enjoy."

"But nothing stable can be built upon such an unhealthy foundation of self-deception!" Cameron protested.

"It is not unhealthy—not at the present moment," said Venor. "The time will come when it, too, will be thrust aside and a tremendous effort of scholarship will extract the elements of truth and find that which was suppressed. But the Markovians themselves will do it—a generation of them who can afford to laugh at the fears and fantasies of their ancestors."

"This tells us nothing of how you were able to make a creative people out of a race of pirate marauders," said Cameron.

"I gave you the key," said Venor. "It was one used long ago by your own people before it was abandoned.

"How was the savage wolf tamed to become the loyal, friendly dog? Did ancient man try to exterminate the wolves that came to his caves and carried off his young? Perhaps he tried. But he learned, perhaps accidentally, another way of conquest. He found the wolf's cubs, and learned to love them. He brought the cubs home and cared for them tenderly and his own children played with them and fed them and loved them.

"It took time, but eventually there were no more wild wolves to trouble man, because he had discovered a great friend, the dog. And man plus dog could handle wolf with ease. Dog forgot in time what his forebears were and became willing to defend man against his own kind—because man loved him.

"It happened again and again. Agricultural man hated the wild horse that ate his grain and trampled his fields. But he learned to love the horse, too, after a while. Again—no more wild horses."

"But you can't take a predatory, savage pirate and love him into decency!" Cameron protested.

"No," Venor agreed. "It is too difficult ordinarily at that level, and wasteful of time and resources. But I didn't say that is what happened. You don't tame a wolf by loving it, but the *cubs*—yes. And even pirates have cubs, who are susceptible to being loved.

"The first weapon was hate. But after learning the futility of it, sentient creatures discovered another, the succeeding evolutionary emotion. It is pure savagery in its destructive power, a thousand times more effective in annihilating the enemy.

"You've thought 'Love thy enemy' was a soft, gentle, futile doctrine! Actually, instead of merely killing the enemy it twists his personality, destroys his identity. He continues to live, but he has lost his integrity as an entity. The wolf cub never becomes an adult wolf. He becomes Dog.

"It is not a doctrine of weakness, but the ultimate weapon of destruction. It can be used to induce any orientation desired in the mind of the enemy. He'll do everything you want him to—because he has your love."

"How did you apply that to the Markovians?" asked Joyce in almost a whisper.

"It was one of the most difficult programs we have ever undertaken," said Venor. "There were comparatively few of us and such a tremendous population of Markovians. We had predicted long ago, even before the organization of the Council, the situation would grow critical and dangerous. By the time the Council awoke to the fact and started its futile debates we had made a strong beginning.

"We arranged to be in the path of a Markovian attack on one of the worlds where our work was completed. The Markovians were only too happy to take us into slavery and use us as victims in their brutal sports."

"You didn't deliberately fall into a trap where you allowed yourselves to be killed and tortured by them?" exclaimed Cameron.

Venor smiled. "The Markovians thought we did. We could hardly do that, of course. Our numbers were so small compared with theirs that we wouldn't have lasted very long. And, obviously, it would have been plain stupid. There is one key that must not be forgotten: An effective use of love requires an absolute superiority on the levels attainable by the individual to be tamed. So, in this case, we had to have power to keep the Markovians from slaughtering us or we would have been unable to accomplish our purpose.

"Teleportation is of obvious use here. Likewise, psychosomatic controls that can handle any ordinary wound we might permit them to inflict. We gave them the illusion of slaughtering and torturing us, but our numbers did not dwindle."

"Why did you give them such an illusion?" Joyce asked. "And you say you *permitted* them to inflict wounds—?"

Venor nodded. "We were in their households, you see, employed as slaves and assigned the care of their young. The cubs of the wolf were given into our hands to love—and to tame.

"These Markovian children were witnesses to the supposed torture and killing of those who loved them. It was a tremendous psychic impact and served to drive their influence toward the side of the slaves. And even the adults slowly recognized the net loss to them of doing away with servants so skilled and useful in household tasks and caring for the young. The games and brutality vanished spontaneously within a short time. Markovians, young and old, simply didn't want them any longer.

"During the maturity of that first generation of young on whom we expended our love our position became more secure. These were no longer wolves. They had become dogs, loyal to those who had loved them, and we could use them now against their own kind. Influences to abandon piracy against other peoples began to spread throughout the Nucleus.

"Today the Markovians are no longer a threat capable of holding the Council worlds in helpless fear. They long ago ceased their depredations. Their internal stability is rising and is almost at the point where we shall be able to leave them. Our work here is about finished."

"Surely all this was unnecessary!" Joyce said. "With your powers of teleportation and other psionic abilities you must possess it should have been easy for you to *control* the Markovians directly, force them to cease their piracy—"

"Of course," said Venor. "That would have been so much easier for us. And so futile. The Markovians would have learned nothing through being taken over by us and operated externally. They would have remained the same. But it was our desire to change them, teach them, accomplish genuine learning within them. It is always longer and more difficult this way. The results, however, are more lasting!"

"*Who* are you people—*what* are you?" Cameron said with sudden intensity. "You have teleportation—and how many other unknown psychic powers? You have forced us to believe you can tame such a vicious world as the Markovian Nucleus once was.

"But where is there a life of your own? With all your powers you must live at the whim of other cultures. Where is *your* culture? Where is your own purpose? In spite of all you have, your life is a parasitical one."

Venor smiled gently. "Is not the parent—or the teacher—the servant of the child?" he said. "Has it not always been so if a species is to rise very far in its conquest of the Universe?

"But this does not mean that the parent or teacher has no life of his own. You ask where is our culture? The culture of *all* worlds is ours. We don't have great cities and vast fleets. The wolf cubs build these for us. They carry us across space and shelter us in their cities.

"Our own energies are expended in a thousand other and more profitable ways. We have sought and learned a few of the secrets of life and mind. With these we can move as you were moved, when we choose to do so. From where I sit I can speak with any of our kind on this planet or any world of the entire Nucleus. And a few of us, united in the effort, can touch those in distant galaxies.

"What culture would you have us acquire, that we do not have?" Venor finished.

Without answer, Cameron arose and strode slowly to the window, his back to the room. He looked out upon the rude wooden huts and the towering forest beyond. He tried to tell himself it was all a lie. Such things couldn't be. But he could feel it now with increasing strength, as if all his senses were quickening—the benign aura, the indefinable wash of power that seemed to lap at the edge of his mind.

Out of the corner of his eye he could see Joyce's face, almost radiant as she, too, sensed it here in the presence of the Ids.

Love, as a genuine power, had been taught by every Terran philosopher of any social worth. But it had never really been tried. Not in the way the Ids understood it. Cameron felt he could only guess at the terrible discipline of mind it required to use it as they did. The analogy of the wolf cubs was all very well, and man had learned to go that far. But there is a difference when your own kind is involved, he thought.

Perhaps it was out of sheer fear of each other that men continued to try to sway with hate, the most primitive of all their weapons.

It's easy to hate, he thought. Love is hard, and because it is, the tough humans who can't achieve it and have the patience to manipulate it must scorn it. The truly weak ones, they're incapable of the stern and brutal self-discipline required of one who loves his enemy.

But men had known how. Back in the caves they had known how to conquer the wolf and the wild horse. Where had they lost it?

The vision of the buildings and the forest with its eternal peace was still in his eyes. What else could you want, with the whole Universe in the palm of your hand?

He turned sharply. "You tricked us into betraying ourselves to Marthasa, and you said that you planned it this way when you first heard of our coming. But you have not yet said why. Why did you want us to see what you had done?"

"You needed to have evidence from the Markovians themselves," said Venor. "That is why I led you to the point where the admission would be forced from them. The problem you came to solve is now answered, is it not? Is there anything to prevent you returning to Earth and writing a successful paper on the mystery of the Markovians?"

"You know very well there is," said Cameron with the sudden sense that Venor was laughing gently at him. "Who on Earth would believe what you have told me—that a handful of meek, subservient Ids had conquered the mighty Markovian Nucleus?"

He paused, looking at Joyce who returned his intense gaze.

"Is that all?" said Venor finally.

"No that is not all. After taking us to the heights and showing us everything that lies beyond, are you simply going to turn us away empty-handed?"

"What would you have us give you?"

"This," said Cameron, gesturing with his hand to include the circle of all of them, and the community beyond the window. "We want what you have discovered. Is your circle a closed one—or can you admit those who would learn of your ways but are not of your race?"

Venor's smile broadened as he arose and stepped toward them, and they felt the warm wave of acceptance from his mind even before he spoke. "This is what we brought you here to receive," he said. "But you had to ask for yourselves. We wanted men of Earth in our ranks. There are many races and many worlds who make up the Idealists. That is why it is said that the Ids do not know the home world from which they originally came. It is true, they do not. We are citizens of the Universe.

"But we have never been represented by a native of Earth, which needs us badly. Will you join us, Terrans?"

www.ingramcontent.com/pod-product-compliance
Lightning Source LLC
Chambersburg PA
CBHW030640130626
46552CB00002B/945